MW01363408

The Painted Hills

The Circuit Rider Series, **PART ONE**

DENNIS ELLINGSON

WESTBOW PRESS
A DIVISION OF THOMAS NELSON

WestBow Press books may be ordered through booksellers or by contacting:

WestBow Press
A Division of Thomas Nelson
1663 Liberty Drive
Bloomington, IN 47403
www.westbowpress.com
1-(866) 928-1240

ISBN: 978-1-4497-5929-2 (sc)

Library of Congress Control Number: 2012912373

Printed in the United States of America

WestBow Press rev. date: 09/05/2012

"O wretched man that I am!
Who shall deliver me from the
body of this death?

I thank God through Jesus Christ our Lord.
So then with the mind I myself serve
The Law of God;
But with the flesh sin."

Romans 7:24&25 K.J.V.

All Bible Quotations are from the K.J.V. Bible
of the era of the setting of this story

Permission from Scotty Vaughn to reprint
lyrics to Circuit Ridin' Preacher

Thanks to my wife Kit for her wonderful
photographs and her editing help.
Thanks to my mother Geri Ellingson for her editing.
Thanks to the Flying W Wranglers for a concert to remember.
Thanks to the Heavenly Father for seeing fit to
have me live and roam in the wild and wonderful
places of Oregon; East of the Cascades.

Circuit Ridin' Preacher

He rode into camp one Sunday
While the boys were still around
We'd hardly finished breakfast
When the preacher man stepped down
The boss said, "Light and have some coffee
And some grub if you've a mind."
He said, "No thank, but could I
Have a little of your time."

He said, "I'm a circuit rider
And I go from camp to camp
I'm here to feed the hungry,
And to light the Master's lamp.
To spread the love of Jesus
To those who haven't heard
So gather round you buckaroos
I'll share with the Word."

Chorus
He sang, "What a friend we have in Jesus."
Took a Bible and read John 3:16
"For God so loved the world that he gave His only Son
And He'll save you cowboys too, if you believe.

As I looked around the wagon
I could see on every face
That circuit rider preacher
Had mad a church out of that place
And out there on the prairie
Underneath the mornin' sun
I asked Jesus in my heart
In front of God and everyone.

When he rode off that afternoon
I watched till he was gone,
And many times I wondered
What range he's ridin on
And if he still remembers
When he showed me the way
God knows I won't forget
When he rode into camp that day.

Scott Vaughn – The Flying W Wranglers – Cowboys for Jesus
The Painted Hills

Contents

Introduction

I have lived in the West most of my life. I am a born and raised Oregonian and I have lived and traveled all over this state. My favorite places are east of the Cascades in the Plateau and Great Basin lands mostly made up of diverse High Desert lands.

Don't let the idea of High Desert fool you into thinking nothing but cactus and sagebrush. While we do have plenty of the latter cacti are few and far between, but Juniper, Pine, Cedar, Fir, Mountain Hemlock are plentiful. There are wild rivers, bountiful lakes and sweet streams in abundance. There are always plenty of cold winters as well as hot summers.

I have remained in Oregon and my plans are to make my exit to heaven from here as well. The geography of this area is unparalleled in its beauty and awesome ruggedness. Out in these open places where the sun shines bright and the sky is blue much of the time I can sense the Hand of God. Maybe this isn't Eden but it is Eden for me.

In this Circuit Rider series you and I will find real places, some real people and stories drawn from real times of the era of the Old West. You will meet people who did and could have lived at this historic time. Our central character, J.L. is a man you will find very human but seeking the best for himself. His journeys in these series of books will take you to real places that you can visit today.

The Circuit Rider of old was a traveling "Man of the Cloth". He went forth to village, camp and homestead to share the burden God had put upon him and that to tell and example the love that God has for all His creation.

Each volume of the Circuit Rider will take us to different landmarks of Oregon and beyond. Many of the places described here are real places you can locate on a map and travel to today.

Our first journey will take you to the village of The Dalles lying on the rugged banks of the great Columbia River and the magnificent gorge country the river carved. From there we journey to an out of the way place called the Painted Hills. This is a place of such stark beauty and grandeur that it is beyond my wits to describe completely, although I will try. Perhaps you will just have to see the area for yourself as I have. We will follow along on an exciting adventure through the great lands that make up the Wild West of yesterday and today.

History of The Dalles:

I know the town from my childhood. The name means "The Falls". Those falls no longer exist, drowned in the name of progress in 1957. I can remember as a young boy living in The Dalles, specifically the Chenoweth area, as an area that was filled with adventure. There were the cliffs above the Chenoweth Elementary School. These cliffs contained some shallow caves and in those caves, in days gone by, you could find arrow points and if you let your imagination run a little wild it wasn't hard to imagine what a place that might have been a hundred years before.

I remember going out to a place called Celilo Falls on the Columbia River before The Dalles Dam was constructed. We watched the Wasco Indians fish for salmon off precarious platforms that hung out over the churning river as if held up with no visible means of support. It was the last year the natives would have the opportunity to fish theses waters as they had for centuries. I remember huge writhing salmon being caught in their journey east to spawn and die.

In 1959 I remember celebrating the Oregon Centennial and watching the parade that was to replicate the time of Oregon's birth. I remember and still realize to this day, how blessed I am to live in a part of the country that was part of the legendary "Old West".

We lived in The Dalles before moving on to Central Oregon. I have been back a number of times drawn by its history and beauty. After becoming a Christian and a pastor, I returned to The Dalles to visit an old abandoned Mennonite village. The old village seemed to hang on the rock banks of the Columbia River. I wondered what it must have been like for those hardy people who lived in such primitive conditions. Yet they were ready to share their faith and love of Jesus the Christ in a new and dangerous land; the Oregon Country.

History of The Painted Hills

The Painted Hills, now a protected geologic site and part of the vast John Day Fossil Beds National Monument, are located in the heart of Central Oregon 75 miles east of the City of Bend. As an adult I first visited the Painted Hills briefly on my way east to a church conference. It was just a quick look at what I can only call an indescribable beauty of the process of volcanism and erosion and the left over reminders of the world wide deluge we know as the Flood of Noah. This is a hidden away place, unlike any other place in the West. Rain, snow, wind and time have turned these painted hills into one of the most stunning examples of creation and also the fall of mankind.

Later my wife, Kit, and I returned to try to capture the harsh beauty of the Painted Hills through the camera lens. It is no easy task because the beauty is greater that can be represented by lens or brush. As we looked and hiked we knew that this was the land of deer, the pronghorn and elk but also learned that not so very long ago great animals like mammoths, giant camels and other extinct beasts roamed. The evidence of their fossilized remains can be found in abundance in this vast land. As we drank in this place we also realized that these great places of wild and stark beauty arrived here through the Intelligent Design of an Awesome God who must have reveled in the creation of this once secret place.

Chapter One

Daybreak

"Because of the Lord's great love we are not consumed, for his compassions never fail.
They are new every morning; great is Your faithfulness."
Lamentation 3:22&23

The early spring morning was a cool one; bits of frost formed on the sage brush and the men and horses' breath vapors strung out from their mouths like small shrouds of fog. Along Bridge Creek early morning fog hovered for a bit, ready to disappear as the first rays of sunshine broke between the hills.

"You have to see this in the morning to appreciate His handiwork best, J.L.," said the old man.

"Well, the only one up right now ought to be Him. The rest of us could use a little more sleep." J.L. grumbled and yet kidded at the same time. "And we haven't even had coffee yet," he decided to add as he let off a shiver against the cold and shrugged a little deeper into his old, worn army coat.

Inside, however, J.L. felt warmth. It was a different kind of warmth than he had ever felt before. This was something akin to a peace or a satisfaction that somehow things would work out. Again this feeling brushed by him and he couldn't explain it but he appreciated it. As he looked around he had to admit the old man was correct. This place, as the sun began to chase off the long shadows, looked like nothing he had ever seen before. And he had certainly seen plenty of hills and mountains in his life time.

He had lived in the pastoral Appalachians of Virginia and had experienced the terrible bloody hills and knolls of Gettysburg. He had come through the Rockies and never imagined mountains so high that they seemed to push against the sky. He had seen the Sawtooths, the Seven Devils and the large rolling bare hills far in Eastern Oregon that seemed to go on forever. He had been in the forested Cascades and peered at the snowy splendors of Mt. Hood, Jefferson and Adams to the West. But these hills were different. They weren't mountains hut hills that seemed as if an artist with a great palette of color and a fine brush painted violets, reds, rust, tan and whites in great horizontal strokes. The colors seemed to grow more brilliant as the sun grew bright on that cool spring morn.

J.L. wondered how many others had ventured through the winding creek canyon to witness theses painted hills, certainly not many white men, 'cept some trappers or the frontiersmen of old. Maybe some of those few that lived close by. 'How did the old man find his way into this place that was not so easy to be found?' J.L. had wondered to himself.

As the sun marched higher into the morning sky, a new set of colors began to emerge on the hills. These colors, like fine veins of gold chipped away from rock and revealed as if by a lucky miner, ran up and down the hills in jagged ways with the shape of the nooks and crannies of these ancient hills.

The two men stopped their horses to sit and stare as the sun continued to rise. Gus, J.L.'s horse, snipped at bits of grass apparently appreciating the stop. The old man's great black dog was busy sniffing at the brush in case there might be something he could flush out and chase. It was still cold and the dawning presence of sun was still not great enough to shake off the freezing temperature. J.L. noticed that the old man next to him was shivering in his black frock coat. He shrugged off his coat and from his horse draped it across the old man's shoulders without saying a word. He was younger, he thought and could bear the cold for awhile until the sun's warmth reached body and bone.

The two men continued to look at the hills which seemed to change in color and hue from moment to moment as the new day's sunrise advanced. And then there was what looked like veins of gold tracing through the hills. These veins became brighter in the morning sun and J.L. thought to dismount and see this close for himself.

It was if the old man knew what J.L. was thinking, "Gold miners would think they had found the mother lode if they saw this, but this is a different kind of gold that only lasts for a while and then withers and dies and blows away in the wind," he poetically noted indicating that these veins of gold were but wildflowers present for a few weeks but no less glorious.

As he listened to the old man, J.L. felt like there might be another exhortation coming on from him. He had heard a number of them over the days they had been together and on a morning like this, even though he hadn't had his coffee, he would have welcomed another one.

Suddenly, though, there were new sounds that broke the peace of that moment and changed J.L.'s life forever. They were sounds that he had heard before and a long time back. They were sounds that prompted immediate fear and a rush of adrenaline and they were sounds he would never have wanted to hear again especially in this heavenly place.

J.L., as in past experiences, could not tell what he heard first. There was the sound of a loud thump as if a heavy rock had been dropped upon a hollow log. There was a deep but quick groan that he realized did not come from him. Then, almost too far away to be heard was the sound of the discharge of a large rifle, perhaps a Sharps. He turned to look at the old man to see if he had heard the same thing. The old man looked confused or maybe more stunned and still as if frozen in the saddle but for only a moment. Then slowly, as a tall tree would topple, the old man fell to the left and away from J.L., off his horse. He did nothing to stop himself from the fall and J.L. could not grab him in time.

At that movement the old man's horse jumped which in turn caused Gus to shimmy and snort. Then there was another sound and that of a cruel singing as another large slug passed very close by and then the awful sound of explosion of hammer upon primer and primer upon gunpowder.

J.L. jumped for the ground while at the same time pulling his rifle from the scabbard. The horses shimmied and shayed around him and the old man groaned lightly and seemed to be trying to say something. J.L. lay prone like a soldier at aim, rifle up and ready. He tried to focus in with the scope judging where he thought the shots had come from. He looked here, looked there, cocked the rifle ready to protect and avenge, but yet he saw nothing. Dust from the horses' hooves stirred and clouded the spot and he tried to keep it from his eyes.

He kept looking but all he saw was sage and juniper and shadows. 'Wait,' he thought in the moment, 'what was that just off to his left, hundreds of yards away?' He tried to sight it, a flash of blurred color from perhaps a coat moved over the crosshairs of his scope. He fired off a shot even though he knew the mark was probably too far for his 30-30. As the flash of that coat disappeared behind a tree or a shadow, he did not know what; he did know he had seen it before, touching a recent and unpleasant memory.

J.L. heard the old man groan and he seemed to be calling out his name. Had he told him his true name?

"John Luke, John Luke," whispered the old man.

J.L. crawled to him, but kept his eye on where he had seen the one who had apparently fired the shots. The old man was gray and pale and looked as if death was upon him.

"It's alright, I am right here, stay still, you don't have to talk, I will help," J.L. said trying to comfort him, as he gathered the old man in his arms cradling him. The big black dog lay by the man, nearly on top of him until J.L. pushed him to the side.

The old man, however, kept talking, "John Luke, John Luke, 'forgive them for they know not what they do.'" The old man seemed to hardly have a breath left in him but again he spoke in a barely discernable voice, "John Luke, 'I am with you always, even unto the end of the world.' John Luke, 'my peace I leave with you.'" And then the old man became silent except for one last long breath exhaled. This was a sound J.L. had heard too many times before, the sound that announced the end of a life.

Now all became still just as the peaceful sunrise minutes before. The grand scene still gleamed in the morning light but the old man was dead. The murderer was not to be seen. The peaceful feeling of just minutes ago was now covered as if by a dark shroud put upon the scene by the devil himself in these Painted Hills.

* * *

J.L. didn't know how long he had stayed there with the old man lying cradled in his arms. Time seemed to stop or maybe didn't exist at all. He would look at the old man. Though he was old he had been so full of life and so full of words too that had stopped J.L. in his tracks and made him think. It was a strange scene; here was the old man dead, gray head rolled back, J.L. trying to pull his old army coat tighter around the man as if somehow that would help. And J.L. did something he hadn't done since being a teenaged solder at Gettysburg. He wept and wept, tears streaming from his eyes, down his cheeks and even on to the still face of the man he had come to love and respect in the matter of days he had known him.

He wept as if he had lost a father or a mother. He wept as if he had lost a bit of himself; a new possibility of a self he had wondered if it could even exist. And the words, those confusing words of the old man, kept ringing through his ears and in his head and his heart. At that black moment he could not understand them or grasp their meaning.

The sun continued to rise. Ravens cawed in the distance as the world around him came to life in a new day that at the moment felt like winter but promised spring. Suddenly a jackrabbit jumped in front of J.L. making him and the dog start. This shook him out of the shock of his despair. His weeping now ceased and a new emotion began to take over and it was a raw anger and a desire for revenge red as the blood that had been spilt. It was a deep anger, full of rage and something he had not felt in a long time. It was a deep emotion coming from somewhere else that was deeper than what this terrible moment had caused.

J.L. vowed on that morning, spring of 1875, in the Oregon country east of the Cascades that the one who had done this dastardly thing to one so innocent would pay for it all. If J.L. needed a lifetime to find the culprit he would take it regardless of anything or anybody else. 'It would be "An eye for an eye, a tooth for a tooth" and a life for a life. Before his days ran out someone else would die at his hand he thought aloud. I will shout in pleasure as that person's blood runs out leaving him stone cold dead,' J.L. muttered the promise to himself.

J.L. Matthews buried Reverend Gideon Thomas there. He knew little of his family but he would find them and let them know. The black dog named Goliath whimpered and scratched at the new mound of dirt knowing that his old master was there. Somehow though, this place seemed fitting. J.L. also did not want to waste time because his need for vengeance was ready to retaliate and time would not wait. He gathered up the belongings of the old man which were minimal at best; a Bible, a notebook, a few greenbacks, some coin and some handwritten papers.

J.L.'s army coat was as ruined as the old man's body had become by the shell of the large caliber gun that exploded in his chest and shot through the back. There was another black frock coat. J.L. put it on, mounted his horse, leading the other horse behind him and turning his horse's head, he sought for the spot that he could best recollect that he had seen that flash of familiar clothing in his sights.

Once upon that high hill above the Painted Hills, he found little to tell him much but two empty shell casings and a bit of ash from a hand rolled cigarette. He trudged around the area for- a bit and put the shell casings in his pocket. There however, seemed little he could do to search for the killer on that day while leading another horse.

Now he would need to get to his destination even though he was ready for the manhunt instead. The new little town of Mitchell, he reckoned, was but a half day's ride away.

J.L. turned Gus' head, went back down the hill and followed the trail out of the bright hills and followed the little creek up and out of the valley.

Chapter Two

A Life Gone Awry

"Wine is the mocker, strong drink is raging:
And whosoever is deceived thereby is not wise."
Proverbs 20:1

Six weeks earlier the sun had shined squarely in J.L.'s punished face, forcing him to awake even though the alcohol induced sleep sought to keep him unconscious. For a brief moment, as J.L. tried to shield his eyes from the bright sun, it seemed like it was just another morning waking in the bunk house he had called home for these last three months. But then there was the riveting pain through out his body that reminded him that he had not bedded down early like he told himself he should. Instead there had been liquor and trouble.

"Did I fight?" He asked no one in particular.

Dapper Dave, close by answered, "Yes, you did."

"Did I win?" J.L. asked back. This was not a new conversation. J.L. and Dave or others in the bunk house had talked this before.

"Let the mirror tell you if you think you won or not." Dave replied.

J.L. groaned and tried to cover his eyes with his hand to block the sun but any movement brought searing pain.

"I think you went too far this time, J.L. The boss wants to talk to you. He said as soon as you were awake you needed to go see him." Dave added.

J.L. moved to the side of the bunk and dropped his legs over the side. Everything hurt. His knuckles were bruised and when he rose up his head and face ached and there was a dull ache that seemed to encompass his whole midsection.

'I have got to stop this!' he told himself. 'Enough is enough.' He had told himself this time and time again and on a more frequent rate since Maddie had tossed him out. He had come to live and work at the Flying High Ranch.

He made it up from the bed and staggered across the wood floor of the bunk house towards the door. But he became light-headed and crumpled to the ground. He lay there for a moment and reached out for Dave's extended hand. Dave did his best to yank the big man back up on his feet.

Once through the door and outside in the cold March air, the freshness of it helped J.L. to chase the alcohol induced cobwebs away. He went to the wash basin, filled it full of cold water, poured it over his head and vigorously rubbed his face and hands despite the pain. Though the pain was terrible, he felt a little revived, though the nauseous feeling in the pit of his stomach wouldn't go away. He went on over to the main house, unaware of the time and not even sure what day it was.

The boss, Jonah High, was heading out the door with his wife and children. The family was dressed in their Sunday best. J.L. concluded that this was Sunday and that they were on their way to church. Church, he remembered it well, his family always went when he was a child. And Maddie insisted on going when they were married. As for him, he could take it or leave it but given the chance he would leave it.

"Mornin' boss, ma'am, ladies." J.L. said, trying to be upbeat and showing that he was really not worse for wear.

"J.L." said Jonah, "I only have a minute, but what I have to say will only take that long." The family continued on to the surrey ignoring J.L.

"J.L. you are a hard worker, you get things done and it is always done right. You don't complain and I am obliged to you for that. And I consider you my friend, but that whiskey you can't seem to do without is ruining you. That was a terrible fight last night. There was damage at the saloon. I paid for it out of my own pocket because you are a good worker and a friend but I can't take a chance with you anymore and I can't risk my reputation on you anymore. You need to be thinking about what Maddie said. There she is at home and your son and you here and acting like some young buck who hasn't learned that life isn't about fighting, drinking and the what. I am sorry J.L., but I have to let you go." The look on Jonah's face was stern as well as his words, but not without caring.

J.L. started to try to explain but knew in his heart that the boss was right. He had nobody to blame but himself. He swallowed hard the words he thought might appease his boss.

"Here is some money, J.L., it's what you have coming and a little extra. I don't have to even do this with the damages you did that I paid for. Do something good with this, make the money count and get your life back on track. If you will do that, you are welcome to come back but otherwise don't show your face around here again especially if it is full of whiskey." His words were hard but not harsh and his face was grim but not condemning.

The ranch owner started to leave but then added one more thing. "You may have really done it this time, J.L. The man you beat up isn't going to let it go. You hurt him badly and he may be the kind of person that had it coming but when he heals up I am afraid you will have hell to pay." And with that the boss strode off to join his family for the half hour ride into town and to attend church.

J.L. felt a heavy weight descend upon him and the nausea that was churning in his gut won and he fell to his knees and retched out the whiskey that had gotten him in the mess he was now in. Dave came along side after the sickness subsided and helped J.L. to his feet again.

"Come on let's get some coffee in you, maybe a little food and we'll talk." Dave was a good friend and one who seemed to know when to stop drinking, something J.L. couldn't seem to do.

Sitting on the porch of the bunkhouse J.L. drank sparingly of the coffee and nibbled on a sourdough biscuit, just enough, he hoped, to keep the nausea away. "Tell me about last night." He said, "I don't remember much but some big son of a gun in a red plaid jacket that seemed to want trouble."

"Oh, he wanted trouble alright. He came to town looking for it and you answered the call and pretty soon you two were fighting. It was hard to tell who would win and the saloon took a beating in the process. But you did him bad. You were getting the best of him and he went for a knife that he had in his boot and it looked like he was going to cut you to ribbons, but somehow you got his hand in yours, knocked the knife away." Dave said, recounting the story and almost living it again as his voice rose and his hands gestured the incidents that took pace. "But the worse part is when you grabbed one of those brass spittoons, juice and all, and brought it down on his knife hand and not just once, but over and over again until you could hardly tell there was a hand there. I suspect he will lose it or it'll be crippled up from here on."

"Why didn't the law step in and throw us both in the clink?" J.L. ventured.

"I think Marshal James would have but by then the fight was over, the foreman had shown up, you two were spent so there was no fight left in you. But, J.L.," said Dave, peering intently into J.L.'s blood shot eyes, "It is who you beat up last night."

"Who was it, I don't remember enough but he sure was mad dog ugly."

"J.L.," Dave said, as if trying to impart a great secret. "It was none other than Clinton Jeffers and when he heals up he will want nothing better than to turn you into buzzard bait. That is the most hateful man since the devil himself and he won't stop until you or he or both are dead. It is time for you to get while the gettin' is good, while he can't do anything because, crippled hand or no hand, he will come for you and come hard."

J.L. sat for a time, sipping at the coffee, trying to nibble down the biscuit and gave thought to the incident he barely remembered. He was not afraid of Jeffers but he wasn't going to be stupid either. After a while he gathered his things, saddled up his horse and said goodbye to the few ranch hands that weren't out working and then headed out of the ranch with one quick last look at the place that had been his temporary home these last three months. He was disgusted with himself for having ruined this opportunity. It seemed as of late that he was good at ruining things.

'Now where?' he thought. He would have liked to have a long hot soak in the tub to relieve all the pain he felt. Besides that there was tenseness in his neck and back that concerned him that he might have another episode from his old war injury. The shell that the field doctors would never remove from close to his spine was his "thorn in the flesh" he guessed. The fight last night must have aggravated it. The other part that worried him was that in the back part of his brain was the desire to chase the pain away with the hair of the dog; a tall shot of whiskey. He was just learning that those thoughts would get him into trouble.

'So where to go', he thought as he rode along, heading south towards town. He thought about the money in his pocket and then thought that he needed to get this to Maddie and give her most of it. Maybe she would let him stay for a while. Maybe he could take that long soak in the old washtub in the barn. That is all that he would ask for, just a place to rest for the day and the night and a bath to soak his sore body.

A few miles before reaching town he took off to the west. The Columbia River was in view below. The big river ran wild and free and was full of water from the winter snows that had begun to melt. He thought about fishing with his son and the pleasant times the family spent there on a few lazy summer evenings. He missed his family bad. He wished he would remember those things before he bellied up to the bar after a hard day's work rather than afterward when the hangover reminded him of another stupid decision.

He headed into the Chenoweth area, the Chenoweth bluffs before him. A mile later the forty acre plot along the creek that he and Maddie had settled 5 years before came into view. It still wasn't much, a small house – more a cabin really, a barn, corrals, some fencing but it had been their home together.

As he rode into the front yard he noticed that the wagon was not there. 'That's right,' he thought, 'it is Sunday and Maddie would be at church'. He would take the opportunity to heat up some water on the stove in the barn, fill up the tub and take a good soak before Maddie returned. She would normally stay in town for the day, usually having dinner with one of her town folk friends. He could be done and gone before she got home. He would leave the money on the kitchen table and maybe a little note too.

He got down from his horse, pulled off the saddle, gave old Gus some hay and grain. There wasn't very much firewood split so he got to chopping for Maddie and what he needed to heat up the stove in the barn. This day, in his hung-over condition, the work was hard but he thought maybe the chopping would help chase off the hangover and loosen up stiff muscles. But then it happened like had happened before. The slug moved just enough in his back to send excruciating shooting pains up into his neck and down into his back all the way into his legs and J.L. crumpled to the ground barely able to move and able to do little but lie in the cold dirt and moan in pain.

* * *

Maddie and Jacob had wanted to stay in town longer that day, after church, but there just seemed so much to do with J.L. gone. So she had a quick dinner with friends and she and her ten year old son headed back the half hour drive home so as to have time to get wood in, animals fed and all of the other chores that seemed to pile up and never all quite get done. Plus she needed to check on in on old Mr. Martin, her neighbor down the way. She had been looking after because of a stroke. It was money that she begrudgingly took from the old gentleman but money he was happy to spend to have the help.

As Maddie and Jacob entered into the compound she noticed that J.L.'s horse was there. As much as loved her husband he was the last person she wanted to see today. While in town she had heard about the fight he had gotten into. She shuddered again thinking about that scoundrel Jeffers he'd had the fight with. She was afraid for him. 'So why was J.L. here and where was he?' she wondered. She looked toward the barn and didn't see him. The house seemed quiet. Then, out of the corner of her eye and to her ear as well, she heard a familiar groan. J.L. laid crumpled in the shade of the woodshed. She jumped from the wagon and walked briskly to where J.L. laid. As she approached the stink of whiskey reached her first and she was ready to lecture him and tell him to get out. But as she got closer she realized her estranged husband was in great pain and unable to move on his own. She knew about the war injury and had fingered the deep scar that ran along the middle of his back. She did not know how long he had laid there but he was shivering and cold. She told Jacob to get some wood burning in the old stove to heat up water. Then half dragging and half carrying the big man she moved J.L. into the barn and wrapped him in horse blankets while she heated water to near boiling and then poured kettle after kettle into the tub.

She pulled all of J.L.'s clothes off except the long-handles he wore at this time of year. Then dragging and pulling at him she put him into the tub.

Finally J.L. began to warm in the hot water of the old tub. The tenseness and pain began to ease and he could think and move again. Maddie was now busy with feeding the animals trying to ignore and not look at him.

J.L. got out of the tub, feeling self-conscious dripping wet in his long underwear. Maddie had brought towels and a full change of clothing that were still in the house. J.L. dried and dressed quickly.

"I wanted to bring you some money, Maddie," J.L. started. "I got paid and a little extra too." He tried to sound upbeat and hoped that Maddie hadn't heard about last night but the look in her eyes faded his hope quick.

If she could have spit vinegar with her words this would have been the time. "John Luke Mark Matthews, you are 33 years old and you are out acting like some young buck half your age who needs a stern talking to and maybe a whipping too. What are you doing and what are you thinking? I am not sure you are thinking at all!" Her hands were on her hips and she was defiant in her words as if she had saved them up for a long time.

"Tell me this if you will! How do I explain your actions to your son? How do I tell him that you're drinking and fighting mean more to you than he does? I swear you are living proof that there are more donkeys' behinds in this world than there are donkeys!"

"Saturday night, the place for a father is to be with his family. We should be sharing stories, singing songs, reading from the Good Book, having time together after a long week of working hard together. Instead you're out spending money on liquor and fighting and spending time with a bunch of no-gooders who should be accepting responsibility for being men themselves. Grow up John! Stop the drinking look what you have done to us!"

Her words grew louder almost to a wail. Her auburn features turned an angry red. "Look what you have done!!" she repeated.

The look on Maddie's face said she wanted to say more and certainly she had the right but she grew quiet, very quiet, and J.L. thought that if she hadn't been so mad she might have started crying. J.L. looked down, mostly at the ground or the water in the tub. He knew he could say nothing and he knew everything she said was true and he had it coming. And the silent moments passed and he wished he could just disappear into the ground.

"You are welcome to stay the night in the barn, but only tonight. And you are to be gone before day beak." She was much quieter now, composed and stating her points in a controlled manner. "But you need to think about this and I won't tell you again. I will never divorce you unless you decide to take up with another woman but you will never step foot on to this property again unless you're clean, clearheaded and not stinking of whiskey. So if you ever hope to have your family again then you better decide what is most important. And one last thing; I love you. I suppose I always will, John, but I sure don't like what you have become. Do you understand me, John?"

"Understood," said J.L., almost in a whisper, the words sticking in the back of his throat. "And, here, here's some money." John handed her most of what he had earned but kept a few dollars back for himself. She took the money, didn't thank him or look at him again and then swept out of the barn into the growing night.

A little later, Jacob showed up with a plate full of dinner. It was steaming and the aroma of Maddie's cooking reminded J.L. of the days before the drinking had gotten away from him. He tried to talk with his son but young Jacob had nothing to say but, "Here," handed the plate to him and then turning on his heal he was back out of the barn.

He was hungry and wolfed the food down appreciating how good a home cooked meal could taste. But the meal made him realize even more what he had lost. Afterward he packed hay together in one of the stalls, took the horse blankets from before and made himself a bed. He thought, 'I will never sleep,' and prepared for a night of feeling bad and guilty but soon he was asleep, snoring softly along with the horses.

Chapter Three

The Promised Land

"If the Lord delights in us, then he will bring us into this land
And give it us a land that floweth with milk and honey."
Numbers 14:8

It seemed like no quicker had J.L. fallen asleep that the dreams began. These were similar dreams, happening many nights out of the week, unless the liquor from that night had dulled him so much that he didn't remember them. First there were the dreams of being home in Virginia, on the farm with his parents. These were the pleasant dreams, snippets of real life mixed in with the unreality of dreams.

There was the farm backed by the green and lush Appalachians. His mother and father were there, God fearing parents who sought to raise him right. There also was his brother, Daniel, older by two years and his two little sisters, Sarah and Hannah. The old farm always seemed so nice draped in sunshine and surrounded by the green hills of the Appalachians. There were the hounds barking, the little girls toting around cats or lambs or piglets or some critter. There were the numerous neighbors who stopped by bringing this or borrowing that. Nobody ever seemed to have money but there seemed to be plenty of life and living to have.

There was the old white church that the family rarely missed a Sunday attending and any other day something was planned. He and is older bother, full of mischief, were always up to something, "Tiny," Danny would say, "let's do this, this'll be fun . . ." and another adventure that would usually get them into trouble would begin. Even though his brother was two years older, J.L. was nearly a head taller than him and so J.L. got the nickname of "Tiny" from his brother. J.L. was the tall, strong one that seemed to stand out in a crowd whether he wanted to or not, getting the credit or the blame as the case may be.

This pleasantness of his dream would go on for a while but pretty soon there would be soldiers and fighting and Gettysburg and then Andersonville. All this seemed to be drenched in blood and cloaked in death. Finally, before he would wake in a cold sweat, there were the searing scenes of his home being burned to the ground. The dreams would torment him as he tossed and turned, mumbled, yelled and sometimes screamed. When he was with Maddie, she was there to comfort him with a cool cloth and a reassuring word. In the bunk house there were complaints and grumbling but a sense of concern from some of the other cowboys who had seen war or had been in that Great War or perhaps harrowing fights with the natives.

The war had been over for him for ten years, but not on many nights and even sometimes images from no where would flash at him during the day. It went on again and again and the horror of it never seemed to cease.

J.L. woke cold and shivering as dawn was beginning to break. He got up, gathered his things and shook off the cold by putting on his old army coat. Physically he did feel somewhat better this morning and his body was not quite so stiff and sore.

It was Monday morning and J.L. was thinking that he needed to get busy and find some work. He saddled and mounted Gus, took a long look around the place Maddie and he had built. What had been his home was not now but it could be again he thought. 'Some how I need to start making things right,' He said to himself.

It was time to stop the drinking. He would just be stronger, develop a will-power to stay away from it or try to be more careful. He could do that, he thought. He could control his drinking. He didn't need to do this. Other people could learn to drink a little and not get drunk. In this bright early spring morning things seemed a little more promising.

J.L. was resolved, he would find some work and he could make things right. He was willing to do about anything. Determined to make a new start, J.L. headed toward The Dalles, a few miles away. Soon he could see the wide Columbia River off to his left. Across the great expanse of water the great rolling hills of Washington, turning from winter brown to spring green. Out of view today, he knew Mt. Adams was draped in winter snow in the near distance. At times he missed Virginia but there was nothing like the West and it still excited him to think that he lived here, way out west.

Maddie and J.L., along with their two boys, had headed out on the Oregon Trail in the late spring of 1869 like many other young adventurers, ready to discover the grandeur of the West. They had been married for four years and had two boys within that space of time. Maddie wanted a daughter but they thought they would wait for that attempt after arriving in the Oregon country.

They had left their home in Virginian. Headed across the green hills and valleys of Kentucky and then on to Missouri, through St. Louis, on to the city of Columbia and then to the jumping off town of Independence. There they joined up with a large wagon train. And then it was a three month journey of high adventure and incredible hardship that surprised them each mile of the way. Then, sadly, in the Idaho country, sickness and disease struck the wagon train taking a number of lives including their youngest son Seth.

Then only the three of them arrived in The Dalles as September came upon the golden barren hills of the gorge country. As were most of the people of the wagon train, there plans were to carry on over the Tollgate road into the Willamette Valley. But Maddie, too, had been deathly ill and so they thought to wait in The Dalles before beginning that last leg of the journey.

As they waited and rested, J.L. was blessed to find a little work with a blacksmith named Swen. J. L had learned bits of the trade from his grandfather as a boy and picked up what he had learned and helped the local Blackie with all the work the wagon trains, farms and ranches generated.

In the evenings, with Maddie convalescing, J.L. would take off on horse back and explore around the area. The more he would explore and ride the more this wide open country appealed to him. It certainly was nothing like Virginia. In fact like nothing he had seen before. There was the great empty plateau land to the East and the forested hills and mountains to the West. At times he would travel just far enough to see Mt. Hood, Mt. St Helens and Mt. Jefferson in the distance.

There were creeks and rivers everywhere full of plump trout. He would watch the natives fishing from a great falls pulling huge salmon from the Columbia. J.L. began to talk with Maddie about staying at least until spring. She was open to it and had been embraced in kindness by some of he ladies from the Methodist church, who had made it a point to visit her during her convalescence. J.L. had heard about the Chenoweth area, west of The Dalles and was able to find a plat of forty acres along the little stream that they could build a home on.

As October rolled in that first year, with the first signs of frost, J.L. was busy building a one room cabin. Maddie, by that time, was feeling stronger. The few neighbors that were around plus some men from the same church came and helped J.L. Within a matter of weeks that had a home, enough of a home at least, to get them through the winter. As the years rolled by both J.L. and Maddie came to know more about cattle and horses and began to make their living from that enterprise. Maddie would grow a great garden in the spring and summer. At times, J.L. would pick up work with the blacksmith in town.

It was all hard work but it seemed like a very good life, but there were to be no more children. Perhaps the sickness on the trail or the hard life it took to make this place their home, Maddie could never get pregnant.

On the times that J.L. would work in town for the blacksmith it always seemed good to stop for a beer and then a whiskey after a long, hot day. After a while it was the whiskey bottle hid in the barn, or in the saddle bag and the drinking became worse and worse. And, for some reason that J.L. couldn't figure, the fighting would start too. He may have been a soldier of war and did his duty, and he was a peaceful man, but something about the whisky and the company and other ornery galoots would get his dander up and the words would come out and the fists would come up. J.L. would usually win the drunken bouts in that he would be the least beat up. But after what seemed some insufferable times endured by Maddie because of his drinking, she told J.L. to move out of their home.

'I don't even like fighting and I am not even sure I like drinking any more.' J.L. talked with himself as he reflected back. 'It is time to change,' he said to himself with resolve.

Upon entering The Dalles he proceeded to look up his hold friend Sven the Blacksmith. The old Swede had settled in The Dalles before Oregon became a state in 1859 and had a found good living with his blacksmith trade. However, now arthritis had found him and he appreciated J.L.'s help.

"Vaht hoppened to you?" Sven said, upon seeing J.L., as if he was the only person in town that hadn't known about the fight.

J.L. was embarrassed. This is not how he wanted people to know him. "Sven, those days are behind me. I want to be done with that life, and it has caused me more trouble that it is worth."

"I surely hopes you are," said Sven. "How can I help you, my friend." he added.

"I was hoping you could find me some work for awhile and if you don't mind maybe I could stay in the back until I get things straightened out and Maddie let's me come home," J.L. said, but feeling even more embarrassed.

"Vell, sure, J.L. I can do that. There isn't a lot of work now but you can stay and maybe with people a knowing that you are here more work will come. It just gets harder for me everyday," said the old Swede, showing J.L. his old arthritic hands.

That day and through the rest of the week, J.L. was busy cleaning up around the place. He actually drummed up some work and so he had a little money in his pocket. He thought by Sunday he could have some more money for Maddie and Jacob Maybe he'd pay them a visit, do a few thing around the place or at least see them in town. He even surprised himself by thinking maybe he would even attend church with them.

Chapter Four

Revenge

"The soul of the wicked desireth evil." Proverbs 21:10a

In the dark shadowy room lit only by a low burning kerosene lantern three men talked. They sat across from each other, a half empty bottle of whisky on the table. A few chipped mugs and an old deck of cards, strewn out, made up the only decorations of the drab front room in the old cabin. The conversation taking place wasn't about the game, it was about J.L. Matthews.

One man sat, bruised in body and face, his right hand wrapped in a huge bandage. This man upon hearing that J.L. was in town and doing some work for the blacksmith began to hatch a murderous plan.

"I don't want you to kill him, you leave that to me," Clint Jeffers said to the two others that made up his gang of thieves and malcontents. "But you give him a thumping tonight that puts him with in an inch of losing his life. You give him a lesson that he won't forget and that will take him a long time to heal up from. And then, when he is about healed up and thinks maybe things are safe, me being at the end of my revenge, I'm going to drop him like a surprised bear with his head in the honey."

The more Jeffers talked the louder he became, to the point that he nearly spit the words out. He would have liked to have slammed his fist on the table to make his point but it hurt way too much to even think such a thing.

His homely face turning red, Jeffers shouted "Did you boys hear me? With in an inch of his life and then when he heals up, he is mine!"

The two other men, one who went by Ratch and the other Bald Bob, nodded their heads in agreement. Ratch's face showed an evil smile that indicated he would relish this task.

Jeffers was the kind of man who seemed to thrive on trouble as well as his business of thriving off the misfortune of others. Nothing seemed to be out of his realm of evil if it was to his gain. To this point in his life he hadn't plotted murder, although some had died at his hand in fights and duels. Jeffers and his little band of cronies acted as leaches on the community they lived in and its surrounding area. If there were cattle to be rustled, money to be taken, guns, liquor or pretty much anything that could be stolen and sold they took it.

Jeffers seemed to be as slippery as a Columbia River eel rarely getting caught for anything big. He never spent more than a few days in jail for what he did get caught for. Even the Christian folk that prayed for the unsaved of the community had to swallow hard when thinking of Jeffers.

"What you waitin' for?" Jeffers shouted. "The night ain't gettin' any younger," he continued, "go do your deed! Take care of that son of a cur out in the bush where nobody will hear you and do him like I said!"

Ratch and Bald Bob didn't wait around to hear anymore, they left the cabin, mounted horses and headed the short distance back to town with the aim of finding J.L. and doing their evil duty.

* * *

Swen had stayed home on Saturday and J.L. puttered around the old shop. There wasn't much to do. He was feeling restless and didn't know why. It had been a good week but he missed his family much. He had hoped to have contact with them but they had not ventured into town. He guessed maybe he would just show up at the church Sunday morning in hopes that Maddie and Jacob would be fine with him sitting with them. He liked the people of the church, but it seemed at times like they were too religious. He guessed they probably thought little of him although nobody ever said anything.

By the time late afternoon rolled around and he hadn't seen Maddie or Jacob in town he decided to stay in for the night and not venture out. He was about to lock up the place and make himself a little supper in the makeshift kitchen in the back when Dave, Shorty and some of the boys from the ranch showed up.

"Hey, J.L. we wondered where you were, somebody said you were doing some work for ole Swen," said Dave entering the shop.

"Yeah, he was good to me and is letting me stay in the back. What are you fellas doing in town?" asked J.L., not feeling sure whether he was glad or not to see his old cronies.

"Payday," Dapper Dave said trying to look like the name that had been given to him by women of the night, "Time to wet the whistle. Why don't you come with us, have a beer? We ain't staying long, we got an early morning tomorrow."

"Naw, I don't think so; the last time was pretty bad. I think I'll just stay here, but it was nice to see you," J.L. tried to sound resolved but friendly.

"You don't have to drink, just come and play a little billiards with us. I've missed your ugly face." Shorty piped in.

J.L. was in a struggle, he said he wasn't going to drink but it would be nice to unwind a little after all he had worked hard. He just wouldn't drink. "Okay, for a little while, just a couple of games."

Dave, Shorty, J.L. and two other cowpokes, named Brad and Rob settled in with the growing crowd. They shot some pool, told stories and J.L. managed with cups of coffee.

Although the beer looked mighty good. Another round came and the bar maid laid a frosty mug in front of J.L. "I'm not drinking tonight," he said.

"Whoops sorry, cowboy, just force of habit I guess." She said, but did not take back the mug of beer.

J.L. pushed the mug away but it didn't seem he could push it far enough. Shorty didn't say anything but he started in on his fresh mug, "Ah, that sure tasted good, and it will be a long time before we get another. We're moving some of the herd to higher ground so we will be out some days."

That seemed to be the trigger and J.L. grabbed the mug and downed it in one large gulp and his resolve vanished as fast as the amber liquid in the mug did. Before long there were a few more empties on the table. Somewhere in that night, J.L. began to think, before the fuzziness got to him, that this was not his plan and with a new resolve he pushed a half empty mug away.

"Boys, I gotta go," he said. And with that left his friends behind, entering in to the cool darkness of the streets of The Dalles. He breathed deep the cool night air. He wasn't happy with himself that he drank, but at the same time he was pleased that he quit before things got out of hand. 'Maybe things are looking up,' he said to himself. 'Maybe I can control my drinking.'

He headed down the few blocks towards the blacksmith shop. He noticed the stars for the first time in a long time and enjoyed the night outside rather that the night inside the stinking saloon.

Caught up in his thoughts he walked along thinking about new possibilities. Lost in his plans he didn't notice the two shadowy figures. There was one to the front of him, hiding in the shadows of the buildings, and the other, following along quiet as a big cat seeking his prey.

As he rounded the corner that led to the Blacksmith shop lying at the edge of town, Ratch and Bald Bob, one from the front and one from the back, jumped him. J.L. fought hard against them and for a moment it looked like he might make his escape. Ratch, however, was able to pull his pistol from his side, turn it butt up and the barrel in his hand and with a high blow smashed it on J.L.'s head, dropping him to his knees.

Bald Bob then kicked J.L. in the stomach, knocking the wind out of him, leaving him unable to do anything but try to gasp for air. Ratch, now next to his horse which was waiting tied in the alleyway, took down a lariat and hogtied J.L.'s feet. Then jumping on to his horse and Bald Bob following on his, Ratch took off with the rope secured to the saddle horn. He would later laugh about this as a "Sagebrush Sashay."

J.L. could do little but be yanked along by the horse. He couldn't get his breath back. He could only flail his arms in front of him trying to keep the brush from beating his face too a pulp, but it did little good. He thought for sure he would die, with the little that he could think, beyond the pain and his own preservation. The sharp edges of stumps, rock and brush that assaulted his back and legs were more than his mind could bear and he wondered if he would black out or maybe die before this tide of torture ended.

Ratch kept it up for a good quarter of a mile, but his horse was wearing out from the strain and he thought the saddle might come off from under him because of the big man's weight. Finding a secluded spot by some old oaks Ratch stopped. J.L., still conscious wondered if the torture was to end and if he would soon hear the sound of a gun that would end his life. Instead Ratch untied his feet and he and Bald Bob lifted J.L. to a standing position.

"This, you son of cur, is for what you done to Clint," Ratch spat. "You probably thought he'd forgotten, well he's got friends and we are here to you let know it ain't forgotten, not never."

And with that a flurry of blows and then kicks came again as J.L. hit the ground. He would see the stars, they looked the same as moments ago and then they went out and so did the world and he fell into unconsciousness.

Ratch and Bald Bob looked at their completed work that Clint had sent them out on. They looked at the crumpled figure of J.L. like two who had just finished a great job they were proud of, like admiring a new piece of furniture or a house or barn just built.

"I guess that will hold him," Ratch said, nudging at J.L. who did not respond.

"Maybe the ride through the sage brush was enough?" Bald Bob said with concern that they had gone too far, and then added, "I think maybe we kilt him he just hasn't stopped breathing yet."

"Naw, he's a tough one he'll be alright . . . eventually," Ratch said, then laughed at the thought. "Yeah, he will be alright, just in time to get his brains blowed out."

They started to leave, then thinking again, Ratch reached down and found J.L.'s wallet and took it. There wasn't much money in it but enough for a nightcap or two back at the Red Dog Saloon.

* * *

After some time, J.L. began to stir. For the moment he couldn't remember where he was or why and what was that sound that woke him. The stars were still there but dawn's early light was beginning to make them fade. At his first movement he remembered what had happened hours before and was surprised to realize that he was awake at all.

His next thought was, 'I've got to move, they didn't finish the job for some reason and they will probably be back.' But thinking about moving and actually moving were two different matters altogether. What he felt was beyond pain and there was also a dullness in places in his body worrying him that the old bullet had moved permanently causing some paralysis.

However, he felt that his life depended upon him moving. He began putting one hand over another, trying to shimmy his legs and knees. He moved a little but at the rate he was going he wasn't getting anywhere very fast. He didn't really recognize the area that he was in, although he didn't believe he was far from town. It seemed to be a little ravine, oaks and brush around. He kept moving for what seemed like along time, although he was convinced that he hadn't gotten far. But the brush was taller and the ravine grew deeper and he could feel coolness to the air and a smell that caused him to believe he was near water. He kept on for a while longer hoping that if those men came back the brush would hide him.

'A little farther,' he told himself. And then as he reached out his hand again, it splashed in water. He crawled a bit more to find himself in a small creek. He dropped his head in drinking deeply, rested for a second then drank again. And it was then that he felt something he had never felt before or certainly not in a very long time. There was a peace that came over him that he could not explain.

'Maybe', he thought, 'this is what you feel like just before you die.' From deep inside came a memory of him as a little boy listening to an old saintly woman telling him a story about the one sheep out of ninety nine that the Great Shepherd came to get. He wasn't sure what that meant now, but he remembered saying in a prayer that he believed in the Shepherd who laid down his life for the flock. It was getting hard to think. He knew he was slipping back out of consciousness but he kept hearing somebody, or maybe it was himself saying, "Jesus, Jesus, Jesus" over and over again.

Chapter Five

The Good Samaritan

"But a certain Samaritan, as he journeyed, came where he was;
And when he saw him, he had compassion on him."
Luke 10:33

At first J.L. thought maybe a coyote was on him thinking easy pickings, but it was somebody's pet dog licking at him and whining. J.L. peered though swollen eyes and noticed that it was one of the biggest, blackest dogs he had ever seen. The dog was licking at his face.

From a distance he heard a man calling, "Goliath, Goliath, where are you, come here!"

The dog, evidently Goliath by name, kept licking him, and then grabbing his shirt sleeve between his teeth trying to pull at J.L.

"Goliath, Goliath," again the voice, now closer.

At that Goliath began to bark as if to say, "Here I am, I am over here."

Soon there was a rustling in the brush and there standing before J.L. was a large, angular man in black, blocking the early morning sunlight.

Upon seeing why Goliath hadn't returned he said, almost as a shout, "Lord in heaven, have mercy on this poor soul!"

It sounded like a prayer, J.L. thought, which was good because the looming figure made him, in his dizziness and delirium, think maybe the Grim Reaper had found him.

"Your poor man, what has happened to you?" said the man, not really expecting an answer but hoping for some response.

J.L. tried to talk but his whole face and throat seemed swollen so that he could barely utter a sound.

"Don't worry about trying to talk right now, I will get you help," said the man. He then grabbed J.L. under his arms and gently pulled him out of the rivulet. Then reached into a pocket and pulled out a handkerchief and began dipping it in the cold little steam that J.L. had all but laid in. He gently washed J.L.'s face and neck and wiped his hair and head.

With a cupped hand he ladled small amounts of water between J.L.'s swollen lips. "I've got to get help," he said to himself and J.L. To the big dog he said, "Goliath, stay."

And with that the man in black disappeared into the brush. Goliath stayed, laid down next to J.L. as close as he could get. Once again, in his great pain, J.L. felt a peace that he could not describe and then the world was once more swallowed up in darkness.

When J.L. awoke again, he found himself in a bed. It took a moment to figure out that it wasn't a bed that he was familiar with. He had thought at first he was home with Maddie and perhaps was waking from a bad dream. There were certainly enough of them. He looked around the little room that he was in. It was small and tidy; the few things that made up the room were Mexican in style. He seemed wrapped in sheets and bandages from head to toe. He hurt something awful with aching or sharp pains in every part of his body. He tried to say some words wanting to say, "Hello, is anybody here?" But all that came out were grunts and raspy sounds.

A small middle aged Mexican woman, evidently hearing the sounds, appeared in the door way. She poured some water into a clay cup from a clay pitcher that sat upon an old table. This was most of the furniture in the room except the bed and a small chest of drawers.

"Here, Senor, drink a little of this, maybe it will help you to get your voice," she said with a heavy accent.

J.L. took a few sips. "How long?" he rasped out.

"Senor?" the woman answered back not understanding what he was saying.

J.L. tried again, "How long have I been here?"

"Hum, let me think, quatro, a four," she answered back and showing him four extended fingers on her small hand.

"I have been here four days?" he rasped out in disbelief.

"Yes, Senor, four days." she answered back while placing her small brown hand on his forehead.

J.L. immediate reaction to that was to want to get up. He was concerned that people would wonder where he was or then he thought maybe nobody really cared at all any more. He started to rise and waves of dizziness overtook him and he sank back into the little bed.

"Senor, stay, you are bad hurt," she said, pushing him back gently with her hand.

She then gave J.L. some more water then left the room only to appear a few minutes later with a bowl of some kind of soup. She gently ladled some into J.L.'s still swollen lips. It tasted good, some chicken and rice he guessed. He consumed half the bowl and then in mid-spoon fell asleep again.

Almost immediately the dreams started. There he was on the farm in the Appalachia country of Virginia. His sister and his brother were there. They were outside. They all seemed to be older now. His sisters now in their early teens were pretty and becoming young women. His brother seemed to be mad at him and was yelling.

"How can you leave us to fight for the confederacy?" Daniel asked in a demanding tone.

"Because I am a Virginian, that is why, and that is the side we are on." J.L. shot back.

"Well, we are Virginians and we are not siding with Davis, Lee and the rest." Daniel came back.

"I don't want a bunch of Northerners telling us how we should live," J.L. hurled back.

Daniel was not going to give up even though he knew it probably wasn't for any good. J.L. had become so headstrong. "That's not what it is about at all; it is about one man owning another."

"You sound like Pa with that," J.L. snapped back.

"Pa is right and you're just letting your wayward ways make the decision for you."

J.L.'s horse was saddled and a bed roll was already tied on him.

"J.L., Momma and Pa are back in there worried to death about this. You can't just leave like this." Daniel shouted again.

"There is a war to be fought and I am a man and that is where I am going," J.L. responded. He even puffed out his chest as if trying to convince himself that he was that man that he was talking about.

There were other horses and riders there too. Three others, new found friends of J.L.'s whom he had been associating with. They caroused around town and when they could find it, drank liquor, bragged and flirted and basically were public nuisances.

They were brash boys, looking like men but not yet. Full of spit and vinegar but with no direction just tired of living at home, working on farms and wanting high adventure. And fighting in a war as "Johnny Rebs" sounded like that adventure to these boys.

"Come on boys, let's go," J.L. shouted.

The other young men, whooped and hollered and the four of them road off to something they could not even begin to imagine, the horror of war and a war among brothers. "It's Cain fighting agin' Abel, and Esau fighting agin' Jacob," one old preacher had lamented.

When J.L. awoke again Marshal James was there. "J.L., is that you lying in Senora Valdez's bed?" he asked.

J.L. wasn't sure if he was kidding or if he looked so bad that he didn't really know for sure.

"Yes sir, it is. Do I look that bad?" He had gained some more of his voice back and was able to reply.

"Not as bad as when you were found. There was a concern if you would even live. Doc Brown was out to see you and did a grand job of wrapping you up to keep you altogether. But at that time he wasn't eve sure it was you," the marshal continued in updating J.L.

"We only began to put two and two together when old Swen came in reporting you as possibly missing. It has been the better part of a week now since anybody has seen you. Your cronies from the ranch said you left them early Saturday night and nobody remembered seeing you since.

"Does Maddie know all about this?" J.L. rasped.

"Nope, she has not been in town. We assumed that maybe you were with her. But then this fella came in and said that he had fished a nearly dead man out of a creek, taken you to the nearest place available which was with Senora Valdez. She was very kind to take care of you."

J.L. laid there not sure what to say, just trying to take it all in. He didn't even know how to feel except that he was appreciative of what everyone had been doing on his behalf. Also, he was bothered by all of the fuss which compounded a deep sense of guilt that if he had straightened up a long time ago this nonsense wouldn't be taking place. He wondered the most about the man who had saved him. It was all very blurry. He remembered a tall man in dark clothes and a big dog with a name that sounded like it came from the Bible.

"J.L., who did this to you, do you know?" the marshal started again.

J.L. had to think for a moment. He knew and remembered Ratch and Bald Bob. Why he wasn't' sure he wanted to share that information bothered him. He hadn't consciously thought about it but brewing in the back of his mind was a sense of revenge and wanting an eye for and eye, a tooth for a tooth and on his terms. If he kept it to himself then he would have his revenge. And yet these thoughts bothered him too.

The marshal asked him again, perhaps reading his mind and wanting the law to intervene before things really got out of hand and someone died.

"Yeah, I know who it was," J.L. said, thinking twice, "It was those cronies of Jeffers."

"Well, I guess we shouldn't be surprised. If you're even thinking about taking matters into your own hands put it out of your mind right now. You couldn't do anything if you wanted, so you let me take care of this and I will do so." The marshal's words were strong but not harsh.

He continued on, "I want this to end and I will go after those boys and charge then with attempted murder being on how they left you. We get them convicted and they will be away for a long time and justice will be done and served and this whole business doesn't have to go any farther. We can include Jeffers in this whole thing. I'd be guessing they were acting on his behalf because of what you did to his hand. All he could do was call the shots. You get well so you can testify in court."

The look on the marshal's face was determined; he was a decent man who attended the same church Maddie did.

He then added, "It is not my business how you live your life J.L., as long as it doesn't cross the law, but your sweet woman and boy don't need this. They deserve what you could really be like, not what the liquor has done to you. And I believe this, there is a better man in there someplace and probably not too deep to be found. Maybe this could be a lesson for you. I don't know what you think about the Almighty up above, 'cause you haven't done much of a job of looking after yourself, but he has obviously had His eye on you and saved your hide and soul." This time the marshal's words were quieter but insistent in their inflection.

J.L. was swept up by the marshal's convicting but yet kind words. "Thanks Marshal, I will stay put," is all he could say and for that matter do.

J.L. was tired after that and fell back to sleep. Again, as twice before there was a sense of peace that he could not explain and this time the dreams didn't evade and punish him but the sense of well-being gave him some sweet sleep.

Chapter Six

"Vengeance is Mine"

"Dearly beloved, avenge not yourselves, but rather give place unto wrath For it is written, vengeance is mine, I will repay, saith the Lord."
Romans 12:19

Ratch, Bald Bob and Jeffers were working hard to finish a bottle of whisky in the lengthening shadows of the day. A beautiful sunset began to form over the Columbia River Gorge country, not that these three would have noticed. They were busy planning their next evil escapade and still reveling over their handling of J.L.

"Yep, we gave him a sage brush sashay that he won't soon forget," Ratch laughed evilly

"Yeah, well maybe you did it too well; no one in town has seen hide nor hair of him since." shot back Jeffers with malice in his voice.

"No boss, we hurt him good, just like you said to but we didn't kill him," Bald Bob said back, although he wasn't so sure Jeffers wasn't right. "And nobody's found his body yet 'cause he was in plain view so he musta gotten off someplace," he added.

"Maybe he got back out to the ranch or maybe the Swede is keeping him hid or maybe somehow he got back to his place in the Chenoweth," Ratch suggested.

"Well, we'll give it up for tonight," said Jeffers. "We need to talk about what's next. We need some cash and I'm not doing much with this dang hand so we need to come up with something that won't take a lot of my doing. Something easy so you two won't foul it up. Maybe we should take a ride up to Hood River find some poor sap who ain't watching his cows or horses too careful."

"Sounds good to me, boss," Ratch said, as he got up from the chair. "But right now I got to see a man about a horse," as he headed for the door to go out and relieve himself of all the whiskey he had been drinking.

As Ratch headed out the cool air felt good and he actually noticed the setting of the sun to the west. The show lit up the green hills of the gorge and adding color to the big shimmering river to the North. But there was something else that caught his eye like the reflection of light off of metal, like maybe a gun barrel pointed his way.

Ratch uttered an expletive and jumped back into the shanty. "There's law out there!" He spat as he slammed the door behind him and dropping the bar into place that locked intruders out.

Each man dove for the floor and at the same time drew their pistols. Jeffers had the most trouble trying to manage with his left hand.

"You boys come out with your hands high in the sky," Marshal James shouted in the twilight towards the shanty. "You don't want this to go bad for you and you are out numbered so lets be done with this now!"

Jeffers shouted out: "This is private property and you have no right being here, leave us be." None of what he said was true; they were squatters living in an abandoned cabin.

"Yeah, I might leave you be if you had let J.L. be. You are all under arrest for the attempted murder of J.L. Matthews," the marshal shouted back.

That answered the question for the men in the shanty if Matthews lived or not. Not only had he lived he was somewhere strong enough and in enough mind to identify who his attackers had been.

"We don't know what you are talking 'bout, we're just in here taking the edge off the day." Jeffers came back, trying to stall for some time.

"Listen fellas, you're out numbered two to one." That wasn't quite true but did sound good as three of the marshal's deputies waited silently in the shadows with him. "Just come out with your hands up, no one gets hurt and you will have your day in court, I guarantee you that." The marshal tried to reason hoping to avoid gunplay.

To those bad boys' way of thinking that wasn't much of a guarantee, because if it wasn't this, the marshal would get them for something else. They already had spent some time as forced guests of the county. They all knew that somewhere along the line their luck could run out and would be bound for prison.

"Give us a minute, Marshal and we'll be out." Jeffers shouted back then adding, "With my hand like this I need a bit of time but we will come out."

"You got thirty seconds to get rid of the pistols and whatever else you're holding in there. Get that door open and walk out with your hands up or else we start firing. This old house doesn't look too bullet proof so we'll probably get at least one of you." The marshal was hoping for no gunplay on either side and if his words were strong enough maybe he could put a little fear in the men and they would come out peacefully.

"Okay boys," Jeffers said in a near whisper, "I don't think we have any options here. Let's do as he says. Ratch, you first and then Bob you next and I'll be right behind you. I think we can squeak out of this one if we play it smart."

"I don't know, boss, I think I'd rather take my chances with lead flying than sitting in that stinking jail again," said Ratch.

"Now, you listen to me, I will get us a lawyer, I know one who owes me a favor and he will get us off." Jeffers lied.

"Are you sure?" asked Bob.

"Come on boys," the marshal's voiced boomed, "your time is up, give up now or meet the devil!"

Jeffers shouted out, "We're coming, don't shoot, we are doing as you say."

From his vantage point in the growing shadows on a little hill overlooking the shanty, the marshal could watch the door as it opened slowly. He was hoping that the men inside would have had a lantern lit so that he could see better what was going on, but it was not the case. First, he recognized Ratch starting on his way out, looking mean and sullen but hands high in the air. He could see Bald Bob behind him, but not clearly enough to know if his hands were up too and then it seemed like all hell broke loose and gunfire came from the door. Bang, bang, bang the shots rang out and he and his deputies had no choice but to return fire and for a moment the air was filled with lead and smoke. When the smoke cleared two bodies lay by the door, one mostly out and one mostly in.

"Lord, have mercy!" the marshal muttered to himself. This is when he loathed his job, when death came calling. He and the deputies carefully revealed themselves from their hidden positions and crept towards the shanty, guns cocked and ready but there was to be no more fire. And there was also no Jeffers to be found. Ratch and Bald Bob lay dead in the doorway. Jeffers was not inside. He seemed to have vanished into thin air. The sun had set and the little house sitting in the shadows had grown so dark that the marshal struck a match hoping to locate a kerosene lamp. There were two, one on the table and another mounted on the wall. He lit them both and began the search for Jeffers.

At first he thought the place was just a one room cabin and that was all, but on closer inspection, he noticed a curtained off area towards the back that must act as a bedroom. He stepped to open the curtain when his booted foot stepped on metal. It was a shell casing. Looking down there were at least five other shells meaning somebody had spent the entire chamber of a six shooter at this spot. He turned back to look towards the opened door thinking that this would have been poor shooting with no target.

"Caleb," he hollered to the deputy closest to the bodies of Ratch and Bald Bob, "Do these boys have guns close by?"

After a short minute, "No, marshal, I see their guns and they are over here on this bench, they're cool and haven't been fired," the deputy answered back.

"What in the world?" the marshal said, mostly thinking to himself. He entered into the little sleeping room, an old cot up against the wall. Something didn't look right. The cot seemed somehow crooked at one end and the legs seemed higher up.

All of a sudden the marshal shouted, "Deputies get out side and get to the back, Jeffers has escaped!" And with that the marshal swiped the cot away like an angry bear swatting at a bee, to reveal a little door low in the wall that was partly ajar and had been the escape route of Jeffers. The men looked high and low, but where ever Jeffers had gotten off to, he was not to be found. The posse would have to come back with hounds before day break but the marshal had his doubts about such an effort and they would have to hope that another day, Jeffers' number would come up.

There was nothing else to do at the old shack along the Columbia. The deputies had the dead men bound up and draped on their horses. The marshal came back out of the shanty holding the shells he found on the floor near the curtain in his hand. He was jingling them like one might with a few coins.

"Seems like Jeffers wasn't much for his gang," he commented to no one in particular.

"What do you mean, Marshal?" Caleb asked.

"It will be interesting to know if any of the bullets Doc digs out of those dead boys matches with these shells."

"Are you saying that Jeffers shot his own men?" Another deputy asked.

"Well, maybe not on purpose, although he didn't have much to shoot at from where he was. Maybe he did it for a diversion to get away, knowing full well that he would sacrifice his pards for his safety."

"So those shots we heard were just from Jeffers gun and was just getting us all to shooting then?" commented another deputy now understanding what had taken place.

"Seems to be the case and it sure does say a lot about the evil character of the one that got away," finished the marshal.

With that they all headed back into town with little to say. The marshal thought to himself, 'Ole King Solomon was certainly right, for every thing there is a season', knowing today that lives had been spared and yet lives and been lost. And no matter how bad these boys seemed, at one time they were just their mamma's sons, somebody to be loved and cared for. Maybe once even to be proud of.

* * *

That next day, late, the marshal paid a visit to J.L. who looked none the better but was sitting up in the little bed while Senora Valdez spooned more of her soup into his still swollen mouth.

"He eat pretty good now," the Senora said to the marshal. "He be alright, I will take care of him until he is."

"You are a kind woman, Senora," the marshal said and he knew that to be the case. She had become widowed years ago and did what she could to fend for herself, always busy and helpful. She worked in the hotel and café to earn her keep. Her life must be hard, the marshal thought, but she always seemed to have a smile upon her face and a sense of grace about her.

"If anyone can tend to him well, it would be you Senora," said the marshal. However, he wondered to himself how this poor woman could take care of this big man, feed him and all that needed when she could barely scrape by herself. He would see if some of the elders of the church could help out.

"You look tired Marshal. Can I get you some a, agua - water, something for you to eat – some sopa?" The old woman queried.

It had been a long day and the marshal was fine to take the hospitality offered. "Yes, Senora, if it is no trouble, I've got a lot to tell this fella."

The marshal waited until Senora had returned. J.L. shifted in the bed and attempted to talk but the words just seemed to get stuck in his throat. He ached so much it was hard to imagine anyone experiencing more pain than this.

The marshal took some time in the quiet twilight of the little room to eat and drink. He knew J.L. wasn't going anywhere and the soup was excellent, full of chicken and again he wondered how this poor woman could provide this.

"It was a long night and a long day but the men who beat you to a pulp have gone on to meet their Maker," the marshal said, after finishing his soup and giving J.L. the details.

"But, Jeffers?" J.L. managed to rasp out.

"I don't know, he had him a plan all along I guess if trouble came knocking. We took dogs out this morning and we thought they had a scent but then we came to a little creek and the dogs couldn't find it. We searched up and down, a few miles each way but, no, I don't know where Jeffers is. But we will find him," the marshal said, trying to sound hopeful yet knowing that a man could lose himself in the high desert to the east or the forested mountains to the west and be a hard one to find. "Maybe he'll know enough to realize that this place is not for him and will go some where else."

J.L. wished the same too, but he doubted that would be the case and he would feel it necessary to be watchful. He didn't know how far this foul man might take his revenge as he had promised.

"I also got over to your place too, to let Maddie know. That was just a little while ago. She wanted to come right now and see you but I convinced her that you would wait 'til morning. Maybe you might look a little more presentable to that fine woman tomorrow."

The marshal added trying to take the edge off a hard situation.

J.L. didn't want Maddie to see him like this and as much as he wanted to see her he regretted it would have to be this way. During his time of wakefulness a new resolve had come over him. He was going to change and he was going to do what ever it would take to change. He was sorry that even though his new resolve was strong it would be hard to recognize it in this beat up carcass.

"So you stay put until it is decided when you can be moved. You may not be out of danger yet, who knows what could be hurt inside that won't take to being shifted around. We will handle things here with the Senora and with Maddie."

J.L. was grateful but he could muster little more than a raspy "thank you". The day had turned to night and even though J.L. hurt he slept all through the night and way into the next bright morning.

When he did open his eyes he looked at what he thought might be an angel silhouetted against the light streaming in from the little window. Was he still asleep? Perhaps he was dead, he wondered? He tried to shake the sleep away to decide just what he saw. The figure seemed to be crying, shoulders shaking slightly.

"John, oh, John what has happened to us." He recognized the voice of Maddie sobbing near the window.

"Maddie, Maddie" he rasped out.

She came to him, sat barely on the edge of the little bed and placed her warm hand upon his face.

"I'll be alright," he tried to say although he didn't know if it came out that way.

"What has happened to us, John? Look what has happened to you," Maddie said, her voice full of despair.

He could only say, "I'll be alright."

Maddie straightened up and shook away the sadness. "I will take you home, John and you will get well and . . .," then the tears came again and she laid her head gently on his chest. She cried for a little longer then composed herself again.

Her mood now was different. "J.L. I love you and I always will but how far will this pain go for both of us? You are hurt but we hurt too!" she said, referring to Jacob.

"Maddie, I will be alright, and I will change. I promise and I mean it," J.L. managed to get out. He wished she could see his resolve to do as he said.

He tried some more, "I will show you. You don't have to move me now; I would just be a burden. Wait 'til I am stronger."

"How long can you stay here? Mrs. Valdez can't take care of you forever?" Maddie asked plaintively, and as if on cue the kind Senora came into the room.

"Yes, Mrs. Matthews I take care of him as long as needed."

"But how?" Maddie responded, "when he gets his appetite back he will eat you out of house and home and what about clothes and bandages and all that?"

"Mrs. Mathews, you not have to worry, that man, that priest or a how do you say, pastor, he make sure that Mr. Matthews be taken care of."

"You mean the man who found him?" Maddie asked. J.L. had been thinking about the man too, trying to remember what he could of him, but it was all still so fuzzy.

"Look, he gave me all the money I need." Senora Valdez said, pulling greenbacks from her apron. "And he told me if more was needed he get more, but this is plenty."

"Who was this man?" asked Maddie.

"I do not know but he was like a priest, like at the church." Mrs. Valdez attended the Catholic church in town.

"Was he one of the priests from that church?" Maddie asked.

"No, no I never see him before but he was like a priest, wore black, a Biblia in his saddle bag. Said God would take care of him that God look after, what his words, after fools."

J.L. certainly felt like a fool but was grateful that who ever this man of God was that he not only saw fit to save him, but went to such measures to make sure he would be taken care of after.

Maddie and J.L. wondered who this 'Good Samaritan' could be, where he came from and how he found him. Maddie thought about the story from the Bible and she would hope to later share it with J.L. Maybe now, she thought, he would be willing to hear from the Good Book.

Senora Valdez left the room leaving Maddie and J.L. there alone. "I'll be alright Maddie, you will see and I will change."

"I want to believe so, and I am afraid I have to go, I need to get supplies for old Mr. Larson and we need some too. I will come again tomorrow." She leaned over to kiss him, stopped just before their lips touched, thought differently and then kissed him on the one bare spot that showed though all of his bandages.

J.L. was grateful for the kiss from her, of any kind. He almost had to laugh, he must look like such a sight, she'd probably rather kiss a pig. There in those moments he thought and realized how much he had given up and lost for the pursuit of liquor. He wondered why it had gotten this way, how his life had gotten so out of hand. At first the drinking was just fun and a way to let off a little steam. But, as his drinking progressed, it seemed like it was the way to forget the past, the awful past of the time in the war. The memories would come stealing in on him at times where he almost felt like he was reliving the horror all over again. Some nights the dreams would be so bad that it would invade his day and he could do little but dwell upon the memories even while he was trying his best to work and live out the new life he and Maddie were having out here in Oregon. It seemed like a few shots, late at night, when everybody was asleep helped him to ward off the demons of those days, at least enough to sleep.

Mrs. Valdez entered the room again to check on her patient. J.L. was beginning to feel a little embarrassed by all of the fussing she did.

"How long have I been here now, Senora." J.L. said, his voice was getting stronger and he was thinking he might like to get up and see about sitting or perhaps standing and walking a bit.

"Oh, Mr. Matthews, it has been a week now."

"A week, I have been in this bed?" All of a sudden J.L. began to realize the bad odor that he smelled was him self and he wondered how everybody else had put up with it.

"Mrs. Valdez, I need to get up, I need to get cleaned up."

"I don't know, Senor, the doctor was not wanting you to move so much."

"I'll be careful, maybe you can help me."

The little woman against the tall man seemed almost comical as she tried to hoist the very stiff J.L. from the bed to a sitting position. He felt dizzy, weak and sat at the edge of the bed for some time.

"Okay, Senor, you try standing up." The little woman tugged and pulled gently on J.L. as he made efforts to stand to his feet.

As he stood up the sheet and blanket fell away and he realized that all he had on were bandages, plenty of them but not enough to cover his modesty. He tried to grab at the falling bed clothes before it all landed on the floor, as if desperate to grab at the sheets and blankets. His arms flailing plus trying to keep his balance, he accidentally shoved Mrs. Valdez away from him. She lost her balance and fell to the floor and he in turn lost his and fell back to the bed with a groan. They both lay where they had fallen for a minute. J.L. was in pain but concerned about Mrs. Valdez and afraid he had hurt her. Mrs. Valdez with some effort rose from the floor but when he saw her he was surprised to see a smile on her face like she was about to start laughing.

"You okay, Senor?" she asked.

"Yes, I am alright."

And with that Mrs. Valdez began to laugh. J.L. wasn't sure what was funny. "Oh, Senor, I raise four boys, I take care of old men, even give them the baths."

Her point was that she wasn't seeing anything that a mother, wife and someone who cared for others hadn't already seen. J.L. began to chuckle too, although it hurt to laugh but he added quickly, "Well, this is one man you don't need to see."

After J.L. rested again for a few moments he asked Mrs. Valdez to try it again. This time he was able to rise, bed clothes and bandages wrapped around him like Lazarus summoned from the tomb by the Lord.

Mrs. Valdez filled a wooden tub on the porch of the little house while J.L. reclined on a bench in the warm afternoon sun. When the tub was filled with warm water, Mrs. Valdez helped J.L. step in. The bed clothing still firmly wrapped around him went into the tub too. J.L. figured that this was a good way to get them washed and keep his modesty about him at the same time. The water stung much of his body but at the same time soothed very sore muscles and he relaxed in the tub for a long time. Mrs. Valdez brought a large serape for J.L. to bundle in when the bath was over.

She took the bedclothes out, wrung them as much as her small weathered hands could and then hung the bedclothes out to dry. While J.L. rested inside she made up the bed again. Doc Brown rode up in his surrey, just in time to redress J.L.'s wounds that still needed attention.

"Son, you have made a remarkable recovery for one that was all but gone," said the kindly doctor, "but you still need to take it easy, at least another week of rest before you start thinking about going home or where ever you plan on going."

It wasn't exactly what J.L. wanted to hear. He thought he needed to get out of Mrs. Valdez's hair and hoped that maybe he could go home to Maddie and Jacob. His body, however, was in agreement with the doctor and he was exhausted from the trip to the bath and once again back in bed. With fresh bandages, some more of Mrs. Valdez's soup he was soon asleep.

Chapter Seven

"Come to Me"

Come to me all ye that labour and are heavy laden,
and I will give you rest."
Matthew 11:28

The next morning J.L. was up early with the sun. He managed to get out of bed on his own and got dressed for the first time in over a week although the process exhausted him. Mrs. Valdez had coffee made with tortillas with eggs and sausage. It took some effort on J.L.'s still bruised face, but he consumed all that the kind senora could make.

As he rested after breakfast, back in his cot, Mrs. Valdez brought him a folded sheet of plain white stationary. "Senor, the padre, he leave this for you and he tell me that when you are well enough to read it that I to give it to you."

"This is from the man who found me?" J.L. checked with her to make sure he understood correctly.

"Yes, he wanted to tell you somethings that he thought would be very important for you to hear."

With bruised stiff hands J.L. took the paper from the old woman and opened it. He was surprised to find that his hands were shaking and he felt anxious in wondering what had been written. The letter was written in the script of a person used to writing. It was neat, orderly and done with care.

Dear Stranger:

I call you that because I have no idea who you are or how you got to where we found you and what may have happened to you. I do know One who does know who you are, your name, the number of your years and even the number of the hairs on your head. I believe it is He that directed my dog to find you.

You were nearly dead when I found you and I was even afraid to move you, but I had to take the chance. The closest house around was that of the Senora who has been looking after you. She seemed a kind person who I could trust to leave you with. It was some effort to get you out of the brushy creek we found you in and to her home while praying that we wouldn't injure you more, but the Lord was gracious.

By the time you read this letter, I pray that you are well into your recovery. I don't know what happened to you. It appears you got one of the worst beatings any one could imagine. I know of only One who suffered more and that is He who died for your sins. I hope whoever did this to you is found and held accountable for their actions.

I know nothing about you but I did notice the smell of ale upon you in all of the mess and the blood. I have asked Mrs. Valdez to take care of you as long as possible and made arrangements for that. What I mostly believe is that the hand of the Almighty was on you. Even though you took a beating no man should have to take, the Heavenly Father spared your life, directed my good dog to find you and provided you with an angel of a woman to look after you.

I have prayed for you and will continue to do so. I hope that if the Lord allows, I will be able to see you and talk with you in person. But if I am not to do that, I wanted to share some scripture that the Lord placed upon my heart for your consideration. I do this in the belief that while you may be a stranger to me you are not to the One who made you.

"Come unto me, all ye that labour and are heavy laden, and I will give you rest. Take my yoke upon you, and learn from, me for I am meek and lowly in heart: and ye shall find rest unto your souls. For my yoke is easy, and my burden is light." Matthew 11:28-30

May these words of our Lord and Savoir, Jesus the Christ, comfort you and lead you on to a noble life and the heavenly home.

To say the least, J.L. was deeply touched by what he read and he reread the letter over and over again. He especially concerned himself with the scripture section. He had never read that passage before, but then since his childhood days he had read little of the Good Book. He did seem to remember a preacher, long ago, preaching about it.

What he did recognize was his need and that he was one who was weary and heavy laden. He thought about this One who promised a rest and an easy burden compared to what the world saddled you with. For J.L., certainly after that terrible war, the loss of his second child, the liquor and the trouble he caused Maddie, he was ready for some help in his life.

While he didn't understand it all, in that bright morning, in simple words, he prayed for the first time in a long time.

"Lord, I don't know you much but I know that I need you and if you are really there then I am willing to take your yoke upon me." He whispered under his breath, his swollen lips and face moving to the words he prayed.

That was all he could muster to say but in that little room God's peace descended upon him and embraced him and then once again he slept.

When he woke again, hours later, the sun high in the afternoon sky, Maddie was there sitting in a chair close, her hand upon his head.

"Good afternoon sleepy head, how are you feeling today?" she greeted him with a smile.

His smile back to her told her everything. "I'm doing better and I am ready to get out of here. I'd like to come home if just for the day. I need to talk with you and Jacob." His words were stronger and clearer although his still swollen lips made talking difficult.

Maddie had thought long and hard when and if the day would might happen, when J.L. would come to his senses about what had been taking place.

"J.L., I would like that too but there is much that needs to be talked out and I need to know you are ready for it and will know how to respond to it." A small frown appeared upon Maddie's face.

"I understand, Maddie, and I have been thinking about it a lot. I also want to show you something that the man who found me left for me." J.L. proceeded, handing the letter to her.

Maddie read it to herself and J.L. was quiet too, although he had questions about what was written there and who the man was. The room, perhaps even the world seemed so quiet as Maddie read. J.L. couldn't understand exactly what he felt but there was a peaceful presence in the room and as Maddie read, it was like she was reading the words as if it had been written for her. J.L. thought he could see a tear form in the corner of each of her eyes.

Maddie put the letter down in her lap and looked at J.L. straight but with softness in her features. "What did this mean to you, what is written here?" she asked quietly.

"First, I guess, I wondered who wrote it, who this man is that took such an effort to help me out. I hope to thank him some day for being that Good Samaritan to me."

"The people of the church think that he is a circuit rider . . .um . . . you know, one that travels to places as a pastor and ministers in places where there are no churches. There is an old gentleman who has been traveling this area for years and travels with a big black dog and people think that is who found you," Maddie added, and that she had asked some of her friends about the stranger.

"Well, he sure went out of his way for a scoundrel like me."

"I think he probably would have done it for anybody but his letter sure shows how concerned he was about you. I hope to get to meet him too."

"You know Maddie people are the strangest things that God ever put on His green earth. You can have two no goods like Ratch and Bald Bob who do what they did to me and seemed to actually enjoyed it and then a fella like this circuit rider and Mrs. Valdez who seem to just flow of the cup of human kindness."

"The Good Book tells us that we are fearfully and wonderfully made. I guess that I have to understand that we can do great and wonderful things and yet we can do fearful and awful things." Maddie added, hoping to try to give some explanation.

"I guess, Maddie, I feel like I have done both, you know that horrible war changed me. It is almost like it killed anything decent in me no matter what I would try to do right," J.L. answered back. He was looking at the floor as if to even discus those days was a dishonor to himself and the human race.

"J.L. you are a decent man, I would have never married you if you hadn't been. But there is no doubt that something happened to you during that war and maybe now this is the time to find out," said Maddie, seizing the opportunity to talk about what had plagued her mind for years.

They were both quiet again for a moment in the sunlit little room, the shadows were beginning to grow longer.

Maddie started again, "What did you think of the words that the pastor shared from the Bible?"

There were feelings that welled up in J.L. when he thought about those words. He didn't want Maddie to know that when he read those words that he thought he might shed tears, although he suspected that she knew anyway.

"I do feel like the person that needs that rest and I do feel weary, a weariness that is deeper than just a hard week's work; but something deeper than my flesh, blood and bones. It seems in some ways we have been through so much that life just wears you down and out. I would like to think there is somebody who you could trust like that who would pick up your burdens, but then I guess I figure that I should carry my own burdens. That is what men do."

"Do you know who is saying this?" Maddie prompted.

"Yep, I guess it would be the Lord Jesus. I know enough from my upbringing and the times we've been to church together that it must be Him saying these things. I guess I just don't understand how such a thing is possible. He's in heaven and I'm here."

"Let me ask you," said Maddie, taking the opportunity, "why do you think the circuit rider did what he did, just because he is a kind man.?"

"Well, I guess, but what do you mean?" J.L. asked scratching at his bandaged head.

"Can we look at that story about the Good Samaritan?" Maddie said, revealing her Bible from her coat. "I am not preaching at you J.L., although sometimes I'd like to."

"No Maddie, I am not going anywhere, I'd like to know myself," J.L. said, settling back.

Maddie found the story and read about the man who was traveling and was waylaid by the bandits and how two people came by where the injured man lay and did nothing to help and then she read of the Good Samaritan. ***"But a certain Samaritan, as he journeyed, came where he was; and when he saw him, he had compassion on him." Luke 10:33***

Maddie interjected here, "I think this is what made the difference, he had a compassion that was not from just himself, but of God and that is why he cared. In this same way as this minister had on you. God drove him to take care of you."

J.L. was beginning to feel a little preached at but he chose to be careful of his words. "I have seen people do things in the supposed name of God that would make you shudder and it seems as if they were anything but of God, not that I know him much. But, if you say so, I am fine with it. For what ever reason that fella saved me I am grateful and it has given me much to think on."

"J.L., tonight would you think about those verses he shared with you and then I'll come in early tomorrow, pick you up in the buckboard and you can spend the day with Jacob and me."

The room grew quiet once again. J.L. felt like he needed to say something but just uttered, "Thanks."

Maddie got up from where she was sitting, leaned over him and pecked him on the lips and then with a wave and a "See you tomorrow" was gone.

J.L. had kissed Maddie many times but he could not remember a kiss that meant so much as that momentary brush of her lips on his.

Chapter Eight

"The Yoke"

"Take my yoke upon you, and learn from me for I am meek and lowly in heart; and you will find rest for your souls."
Matthew 11:29

The next morning Maddie was there to pick him up. J.L. was dressed and ready to go, having gotten up early to wash up and make sure his clothes were clean and his appearance as neat as possible. Maddie even kidded him about how handsome he looked, telling him he didn't need to impress her but she appreciated the gesture.

J.L. offered to drive the buckboard but Maddie declined his offer saying that he could just rest and enjoy the ride. It was a distance of only a few miles but the buckboard was a reminder of the punishment he had received not so long ago. Although in some ways the incident seemed like an eternity ago.

As Maddie and J.L. approached The Dalles from the east she slowed the horses down as she came to a farm where the farmer was plowing his fields in preparation for the growing season. They stopped and Maddie jumped from the wagon. J.L., like some dutiful dog, followed her. She watched for sometime as the farmer and two head of oxen made their way up and down, back and forth, over the rolling hills that made up the farmer's field.

"What has you so interested in this, Maddie, you've seen oxen plow a field plenty of times?" J.L. asked.

"I know," she said, while still watching the farmer and oxen, "I am thinking about the Bible verses that were shared with you from that letter."

"Oh, you mean ***'take my yoke upon you and learn from me'***?" J.L. had read it so many times he had memorized it although the meaning still was not quite clear.

"What do you see, J.L.?" Maddie asked quietly as she continued to watch.

J.L. thought to himself, 'Well, I guess I will go along with her,' even though he was anxious to get home.

J.L. began, "I think one of those old oxen looks like he has been doing this for a long time and knows what the farmer wants from him. The other one, he seems a might young although full sized."

"Go on," Maddie prompted.

"Well, that yoke keeps them close, head to head and tail to tail but they both have a mind of their own because you can see how that young one wants to do it himself sometimes and kinda fights against the yoke.

The farmer has to snap his whip at him sometimes. The old ox wants to go with the flow and the younger one wants to go his own way."

"So how is that similar to what we have read? I thought about it this morning, stopped for a minute and watched when I saw the farmer out with his oxen." Maddie said, prompting J.L.

"Now to think about it, I guess that I thought that somehow Jesus was like the farmer and I was the ox but everybody knows that you have to have two heads in a yoke," said J.L. absentmindedly pulling of his hat to scratch his head as if that would help to engage his brain.

"So, maybe," Maddie interjected, "the Lord is like the old experienced ox that knows how to go and to go with the flow, as you say, with what the farmer wants."

"I know it to be true, my daddy, when he would train a new ox would side him up with an older more obedient one so that the old one could teach him the tricks of the trade, so to speak."

"I think, in the same way, J.L., that is how the Lord means it. He wants you to come into that yoke with him so that he can be as close to you as those oxen are to each other. And He is there to show you the true way."

The verse that popped into J.L.'s head at that moment was, "For my yoke is easy and my burden is light." J.L. had another picture in his mind and that was on the Oregon Trail, especially through the mountains of the Rockies and other steep places. He could remember the oxen, draft horses and mules straining against gravity and the incline of those majestic and yet at times terrible, mountains as they lugged the wagons across them. Sometimes the wagons would pull the animals back, and on occasion with disastrous results.

Maddie got back in the wagon, J.L. followed her. They waved at the farmer and with a fresh new insight into the ways of God. J.L. thought to himself, 'if that is all the Lord wants him for was a beast of burden, then maybe that was the way to go, he just wasn't sure of the way.'

Soon they came into The Dalles proper and it was a bustling place on that bright spring morning as they drove down Front Street. People they knew waved at them and shouted out their names, "J.L. it is good to see you." or "We've been praying for you." J.L. would wave his appreciation although he felt embarrassed about the attention.

Soon enough they passed through the outskirts of the town. As they were leaving though, traveling west to the Chenoweth area, J.L. felt uneasy, like maybe somebody was watching him but hidden away and wary. He could not put his finger on the feeling. He was not sure when the feeling came over him. Perhaps it happened with a flash of color on the streets or a glimpse in an alley, he wasn't sure. He just knew that he had a feeling of uneasiness in an otherwise pleasant time.

He decided to brush it from his mind and enjoy the trip home and the company of his wife, that person he had known nearly a long as he could recollect the memories of home and childhood in Virginia.

Soon they took the turn that led into the Chenoweth district. There weren't a lot of farms and ranches here yet but he figured the time would probably come. The Chenoweth cliffs framed the scene of oaks and willows just beginning to think about budding for spring. From there to the cliffs, hills and mountains to the west, snow was still visible in the higher reaches.

Then there was their ranch, still more of a dream in mind than an actuality. The big barn, the cabin with a couple of rooms added on, more like "lean-tos", protruding from the sides of the main house. The corral, the well house, horses, cattle, clucking chickens, and the gardens; was this place called home.

He also noticed that things looked like they needed a man's touch. There were things that needed to be done that hadn't been take care of in the months that he had been gone, and over the last couple of years when he had let the drinking get out of hand. He felt an immediate twinge of guilt for letting things go. He thought that some how he needed to start making up for all of it and win the respect back of his family. Today, though, just getting down from the wagon was a major chore. After the half hour ride it was all he could do, with Maddie's help, to get into the house and sink into the nearest chair.

Maddie made herself busy in the kitchen, stoking up the fire in the old stove, putting coffee on and getting corn-doggers and fruit preserves out. J.L. was grateful for the coffee, the ride in the early spring chilled him and he was trying to keep from shaking, pulling his old military coat around him.

"There, this should help," said Maddie, pouring a large cup of coffee and setting the biscuits, butter and jam in front of him. J.L. appreciated the attention but was embarrassed feeling a little like what he thought old Mr. Larson might feel like when Maddie was fussing over him.

They both sat quietly for a few minutes. Things felt the same yet different, comfortable yet uncomfortable. Just drinking coffee and enjoying the biscuits with each other was good enough for the moment.

J.L. wasn't sure how to start he just knew he had things to talk with Maddie about and he needed to make sure she had the opportunity to say what was on her mind.

In mid bite he started, "Maddie . . ." as a few crumbs of biscuit came spilling out. Maddie couldn't help but laugh a little, which made J.L. laugh too as he tried to cover his mouth so no more of the corn-dogger would escape.

He chewed a little more and then started again, "Sorry, seems I've forgotten my table manners. This is all just making me feel like I have really let you and Jacob down and, by the way, where is he?"

"He will be along soon; he is over at old Mr. Larson's helping him this morning while I went to fetch you."

J.L. started again, "I am going to be better soon and I want to start helping out, getting things done."

"Jacob and I have managed," Maddie firmly stated.

"Yes, I can see that but there are some things that I should have gotten take care of and didn't and there is still much to do. I mean you could think of me, for the time being, as a hired hand that you don't have to pay. I can continue to do some work for Swen and come out in the afternoons or on some days when Swen doesn't need me."

"I would appreciate the help we certainly could use it, spring is coming and there is more to be done but . . ."

J.L. knew what Maddie was thinking and interrupted, "I will continue to stay at the shop once I am fit to leave Mrs. Valdez's, which I want to do soon. I feel like a big burden, not that she would ever say so."

Maddie gave him a smile but then a frown showed on her face, "The drinking has to stop, if I smell liquor on you or hear from some of the town folks that you are back at, the door will close again. I hate to have to say that."

"You are right Maddie and it is all right." J.L. admitted.

At that moment Jacob came bounding in the door.

"Look what Mr. Larson gave me!" he said with the great excitement of a young boy discovering a treasure while he carefully placed an old cigar box on the kitchen table.

"Can you say 'Hello Mama and Papa', Jacob?" Maddie chided him.

"Oh, yeah, hi Pop, you look awful. But look here!" Jacob said in his excitement. He began to take out a dozen or so arrow and spear points from the cigar box. Many of them were made with black and even some red obsidian.

"Mr. Larson gave you those?" J.L. asked.

"Yeah, he said he found them long ago when he first came here, up around the bluffs and other places. Do you think these are old?" Jacob explained and asked.

"I am sure they are; the natives were here for a long time," J.L. answered.

"Do you think that they shot animals or people with these?" Jacob asked in curious exuberance.

"That's what they were made for but probably mostly for hunting," J.L. answered again.

"I would like to know what it would be like to shoot one of these things." Jacob said, while pretending to draw back a bow and take aim.

"Whoa, watch where you are pointing that thing." J.L. said, holding up his arms as if trying to ward off an imaginary arrow.

"Those are beautiful, son, that is a fine gift. I hope you thanked Mr. Larson," said Maddie.

"Oh, I did." Jacob said, hoping he had remembered.

"Can you put those away for right now and go out and see if those old hens gave us some eggs this morning and feed the other animals too?" Maddie prompted Jacob, "I need to start dinner and the day is wasting."

Jacob scurried out and Maddie was up. J.L. sat there wishing he could do more than just sit there. He started to get up and head for the door, thinking he could help Jacob or do something.

"Where are you going, J.L., there isn't a sharp knife in the place. Maybe you could see about getting that done for us today," Maddie said; thinking quick about something that her husband could do that wouldn't tire him too much.

J.L. appreciated the chore put before him. He gathered up all the knives, found the axe, shovels and anything else he could think of too and took them into the barn. His old grinder was covered in cobwebs but soon he had it out, oiled and ready. With one foot on the pedal the wheel began to hum and the knife blades began to shoot off little sparks as J.L. took off the rough edges. The simple exercise was today a pleasure.

Jacob bounded back and forth, in and out, of the barn busy with his chores. They both noticed a great aroma from the house that wafted into the barn.

'It was good to be home,' J.L. thought, just the simple pleasures of family, work and a place satisfied him today and he realized how much he had missed out in the craziness of the liquor.

Jacob came and hovered over him, watching as J.L. worked now on the axe. He had decided to sharpen anything he could find that could be sharpened.

"Pa, do you think I could try that?" Jacob asked.

"Sure, but not with the axe, your mom would have a fit if you lost a finger or two trying to sharpen this thing up. You can work on this spade in a moment though."

J.L. thought he would take the opportunity to talk with Jacob. "Son, I haven't been a very good Pa to you for some time and I wanted you to know that I am sorry and that this is going to change."

As most ten year old boys are, Jacob didn't really know what to say. He was mad at his father and yet he loved him, and missed him terribly, but he didn't want to show it either.

"Well, Mom misses you but sometimes she is really mad or sometimes cries too. I try to help but I don't know what to say."

"Jacob, are you mad at me too?" J.L. ventured.

"Yeah," Jacob said, not sure if that was okay, not wanting to be in trouble.

"It is all right, because I have been pretty mad at myself too," J.L. reassured.

"You have?" Jacob said with a look of surprise showing on his young face.

"I want you to know, that it will be different now, by God, or I mean with the help of God, it will different." J.L. stammered out yet trying to be strong in his words.

It grew quiet again, other than the sound of the grinding wheel spinning metal on stone singing out. J.L. then took the shovel and motioned for his son to come and sit in front of him, together, the big man's arms around the boy's arms, the two, father and son, ran the shovel up and down the stone. The two of them embraced wasn't exactly a hug, but it was the next best thing to it for a father and son together.

J.L. then found honing stones and oil and the two worked on putting fine edges on the other implements.

When that was done, Jacob asked, "Would it be hard to make some arrows and maybe a bow, Pa?"

"I think we could muster such a thing."

As stiff as J.L. was, after delivering the knives and other kitchen utensils to Maddie, he and Jacob set out to find some suitable willow and oak sticks to construct a bow with arrows.

J.L. and Jacob roamed the land that was home, along the banks of the Chenoweth. The creek was swollen with the beginning of the spring melt off. Along the banks J.L. cut some still bare willow branches. Jacob gathered some oak sticks that had fallen during the winds of winter.

The two worked on the implements together, whittling out a few oak sticks into suitable arrows, with some stone points tied on with bits of rawhide and a sturdy but limber piece of new willow for the bow. They finished it off with a strong piece of tanned rawhide for the drawstring. Jacob scratched out the shape of a bull's eye target on a old piece of wood and rested it up against a hay bale and the two of them took turns trying out their aim with the newly fashioned bow.

Soon Maddie called them for the mid-day meal, the aroma of it had been drifting their way for hours, making them ready to eat long before it was done.

After J.L. and Jacob had washed up, they gathered around the kitchen table now set with a table cloth and the best dishes saved for special occasions.

"Maddie, is this Sunday, because it sure looks like that kind of spread?" J.L. kidded.

Maddie appreciated the compliment and said, "It was nothing, you looked like you boys were going to be hungry though, all that work and play."

They sat for a moment and then Maddie extended her hands so as to hold the hands of the two men in her life. She bowed her head and closed her eyes as did J.L. and Jacob.

"Lord, we thank Thee for Thy many blessings and this life you give us. We thank Thee for Thy providence and love. We thank Thee for this beautiful place Thou have given us to live. We think of those who are less fortunate than we are and ask that Thou keep us mindful that the poor will always be with us."

Maddie didn't say 'Amen' yet, with the understanding that if the others would want to join in, this would be the time.

Jacob started, "I thank you too, Jesus, thanks for this good food and my Ma who cooked it. And, Jesus, thanks for well, you know, my Pa, 'cause we had fun today."

J.L. had a lump grow in his throat so big that all he could mutter was "Thank you."

The two men of the family tore into the roast beef plus potatoes, carrots and turnips still good from keeping in the root cellar. Gravy and preserves were used in abundance with the freshly baked bread. The two ate like there was no tomorrow while Maddie ate and marveled at how much they could consume convinced that both had hollow legs.

Maddie treasured this moment in her heart too, hopeful that a new day had dawned for the family.

After the meal Jacob helped Maddie with dishes and then was sent out to take care of the evening chores. J.L. settled into a comfortable chair in the front room after stoking up the fire. The sun was high in the early spring afternoon and as good as all of this had been he was tired and still in pain. Sleep, though, soon set in and Maddie was quiet in the kitchen mending some laundry.

* * *

"Captain, Captain, they are coming at us hard. There are too many yanks, we don't have enough lead!" It was a cacophony of voices that rang in J.L.'s sleep. "They are firing on us! They are on us, their stinging us, like bees from hell. I am hit. I'm a goner Captain, save us, someone save us!"

"Jimmy, shoot there, watch for the bayonet." The terrible scene went on and J.L. moaned and writhed in the chair, still asleep. "Someone grab the standard, Bill has hit the ground! Somebody pass me powder, hurry, or we're all dead and gone to hell."

In the dream Gettysburg was a hell of smoke and blood and stench and dying everywhere. Friends and comrades lay fallen left and right, bloodied, dismembered, shrieking and groaning, dying and dead.

The only ones who were quiet in this Armageddon between the states and brothers were those who had already died, their eyes open but looking nowhere, mouths open but never to a utter another word.

In his dream J.L. flailed his arms as if trying to smack away the bees of lead that would do him more damage than what he was already bleeding from. The regiment was in retreat except those dead or too injured to be moved.

Two men from his company grabbed J.L. half carrying him and half walking him. J.L. tried moving his legs to help but only one would work. The pain was beyond anything he could imagine. It was like a white fire in the middle of his back that felt like it was trying to burn a hole clean through him. He tried to help himself and was bothered by a shrieking voice near him until he realized that it was he that screamed in such agony every step of the way.

Somehow the three of them dropped into a little hollow, where trees and a litter of bodies could possibly hide them. They lay still; one of the soldiers named Artie stuffed a dirty handkerchief far down into J.L.s mouth. He thought he might suffocate but it kept him quiet. The three played dead men amongst those who played at nothing anymore.

The advance of blue coats seemed to go on forever, they were in a rout over this Rebel regiment and shouts of victory and vengeance rang out in the darkening day. After what seemed like an eternity in hell itself, the day grew quiet and J.L. wondered if this was to be his final day on this earth like so many fallen around him.

All of sudden Maddie was there, she had a cool cloth in her hand and was wiping his face with it and she was saying, "John, John wake up, wake up, it is alright. You are here with us, the war is over."

She had done this numerous times in their ten years together. She had hoped and prayed that as the years advanced that this would get better but these episodes seemed as intense as the first ones years ago.

"Dammed war!" She muttered to herself while trying to calm the shaking J.L. and then immediately asked the Lord for forgiveness for her words.

J.L. came to, slowly, trying to understand how Maddie had gotten to Gettysburg and the lead bees stopped and he once again recognized that he was home.

"You're alright now, John, it was just those dreams. Everything is fine. You are here with us," Maddie comforted, a cool hand rubbing at his cheek.

J.L. laid his head up against Maddie, bit his lip and suppressed the tears he wished he could let out. Jacob came in, saw the scene.

"Mom, Pop is everything alright?" he asked with great concern on his young face.

"Yes, Son it is fine," Maddie said back in a quiet tone.

But they all felt that until these horrible dreams could stop nothing would ever quite be alright. Maddie worried in the moment, knowing that if there was a time for J.L. to find solace in a bottle, now would be the time. Jacob, at ten, didn't understand but just felt sad and wanted to be someplace else. J.L., however, mustered himself up, trying hard to get his bearings and up on his feet.

"Jacob," he managed, "I am alright, don't worry. It is time for me to head back to Mrs. Valdez." He sought his hat but wasn't sure what exactly he was trying to do.

"I'll get the buckboard, but you can rest for a bit, J.L." Maddie said trying to gently push him back down in the chair.

"No, it is getting late. I don't want you traveling back in the dark." J.L. said, not budging against Maddie's small hand.

"Hey, we had a time today didn't we?" said J.L. to Jacob. "You be careful of those arrows, I don't want your mom telling me about a bunch of holes in stuff that don't need holes." J.L. was trying to do all he could to lighten the somber mood as he plastered a smile upon his face.

"Alright Pop, I promise. Will I see you soon?"

"Yes, Son, you will, I promise it." J.L. said, giving his son a pat on the head. "And, my boy, we will be fine," He said as he lifted his son's face so they could see eye to eye. Again J.L. said, "We will be fine."

J.L. and Maddie headed for the buckboard but on second thought he walked to the barn and then to the corral. "I think I will take old Gus with us, and then you won't have to get me next time."

"Are you sure?" asked Maddie, a furrow showing on her forehead.

"It will do me and that old worthless horse some good." said J.L. tying Gus to the back of the wagon and then throwing his saddle and blanket in the back. He then gave the horse a scratch behind the ears.

On their way back to Mrs. Valdez's the two of them talked mostly small talk and mostly Maddie talking with J.L. putting a word in edgewise now and then. It was good to just talk and not having to be too serious and have to think about the dream.

Once past the town J.L. couldn't help but look at the plowed field he and Maddie had stopped to watch the farmer and the oxen plow earlier that day.

Most things, it seems are easily forgotten, some things, though, are always remembered. J.L. knew that he would never forget that scene. It was something for him to consider, the God of everything being a beast of burden, walking along side us, guiding us and shouldering the heavier load. He knew and understood little more than that, but for this day it was a great comfort.

Chapter Nine

Straight Paths

"Lead me, O Lord, in thy righteousness because of mine enemies;
Make thy way straight before my face."
Psalm 5:8

J.L. stayed for a couple more days with Mrs. Valdez, trying to make himself useful, doing some repairs here and there. He chopped wood, mended some fence and what ever else he could do to repay her kindness, which he knew was impossible to do. On that third morning after a fine breakfast of tortilla wrapped eggs, sausage and some peppers that about burned a hole in the roof of his mouth, Mrs. Valdez and he stood together.

"I can't begin to thank you enough for all you have done for me. You were like a mother to me in my time of need," he said, his arm draped around the small woman's shoulders.

"It was no trouble Senor; it is Jesus` Christo who wants us to do these things for each other."

"Yes, but you went way out of your way for me, just like that preacher man who found me," J.L. added.

"Senor, we are our brother's keepers, and so it is not too far to go."

J.L. wasn't sure what to say after that except 'Good bye' and 'Via con Dios' as he had heard other Mexicans say.

Mrs. Valdez gave him a hug, standing on her tip toes to get her arms around him, and she prayed with her eyes closed.

"Senor, watch over this my new brother, show him Your way. Por Vafore, Senor and help to make his path straight. Bless his little family and fix them back together and, Senor Dios, keep him from the liquor. Let him be filled with all that you have, and Senor, help him with those things that have happened before that make his sleep . . . a loco."

The Senora spoke it all in one long sentence faltering at the end but she knew in her heart what she needed to say. "And thank you, and it is in the Name of the Father and of the Son and of the Holy Ghost that I pray. Amen."

"Mrs. Valdez you are a saint and I thank you for those words and I know the good Lord heard and understand you loud and clear. Maybe He will make me less, how'd you say it, less loco," J.L. said with a little laugh. "You will always be a friend of the Matthews family from now on and if you ever need anything, all you have to do is ask."

And with that J.L. and Gus set out some two weeks after he nearly died at the hands of bad men. It was a beautiful morning in that early April spring as he rode towards The Dalles. He glanced at the high hills around him. He could see both sides of the river, Washington and

Oregon were turning a brilliant green in the early morning sun. It was a sure sign that spring had come to stay. In this high desert country where tans and browns were more the normal colors, spring in these arid places was sweet and to be noticed.

The snow and the rain of the winter season had been plentiful this year and so it would mean good grass for animals and plenty of water for crops.

The Dalles was busy and bustling as he and Gus road in. The only places quiet were the taverns and saloons that wouldn't open until noon J.L. headed directly for Swede's blacksmith shop at the end of town and he made a point of not giving the places of drink a second look. Swen was already busy and he could hear the sounds of hammer on iron and steal before he got there.

"Vell, lookit you!" Sven said, "You don't look so bad for a dead man like they was a sayin' about you."

"Yeah, I'm fine, well pretty much. Don't quite have my strength and wind back yet but I was hopin' some work here might help."

"Yes, there is work for you to do," said Swen, wiping sweat from his brow with a sleeve.

"And can I have my little room in the back too?" J.L. hoped and asked.

"Vell, of course, you help yourself, stay as long as you want," Swen reassured.

"A couple of weeks would be good and then I'm hoping that Maddie will say it is time for me to come home."

"She's a fine one, you do good and it will all be fine, that I know," Swen smiled.

J.L. spent the next couple days helping Sven catch up on the work that seemed to be flooding in as farmers and ranchers got ready for spring. It felt good to be busy and so too with his body. The work seemed to help and he worked hard and yet tried to be mindful of the old bullet still lodged in his back. Towards the end of the day he would ride out to home in time to do some chores for Maddie and have supper with them. With all the work that was coming in he was able to purchase items and materials needed for the ranch.

On one of those days as he was traveling back to the town in the settling night he again had the unsettled feeling that he was being watched from someplace near, perhaps behind and old oak tree or boulder. Gus seemed to notice it too and shimmied and snorted. He thought to investigate but at the same time thinking that it would be hard to find anything in the growing dark. If Clint Jeffers was still in the area and gunning for him, J.L. would rather figure a way to bring him out so that if there was an advantage to be had, he would have it.

The next day, during the noon break, J.L. walked over the marshal's office.

"J.L., how are you farin?." inquired the smiling marshal, rising from behind a little desk and extending his hand. "You don't look too worse for wear and a whole lot better than the last time I saw you."

"Yes, sir I am feeling much better and I've been doing work for Swede this week which has helped."

"That is fine, J.L., I am glad to hear that. How are Maddie and Jacob, are you out to see them?"

"Yes sir, everyday, I been doing what I can, I guess more of what I was supposed to be doing all along," J.L. decided to add, "also, I want you to know that I'm not going to be of any trouble to you anymore. I have turned a new leaf."

"Well, that is fine to hear but you were never much trouble other than that fight you had with Jeffers."

"Sir, that is why I am here," J.L. saw a chair and seated himself. "I was curious if there was anything new in your finding him."

I wish I could tell you that there was but that polecat has made himself plenty scarce. We have continued to check when we can, we've not given up. What he did to you was dastardly and what he did to his own men was no better."

"What was that?" J.L. asked, "I guess I don't remember about that."

"That man would sell out his mother I think, that is if he had one."

Then the marshal explained to J.L. how he had brought fire on his cronies leaving them shot up and dead while he escaped out the back.

"That is dastardly as can be." J.L. agreed.

The marshal continued, "It is one thing to have an enemy but to sacrifice your men is pretty low down. I don't know off the top of my head what I could charge him for on that but I'd like to come up with something. True those boys that about done you in were bad enough . . .well, it just all sticks in my craw," said the marshal as he scratched his head as if it might help.

"Do you think maybe he has high-tailed it out of here, Marshal?"

"I am not a wagering man but don't think I would wager that he did. You need to watch out. He has had nearly a month for his hand to heal up some and I would be watching over my shoulder a bit. Keep on to your new life and all and it won't hurt you to call upon the Good Lord for His protection."

With that J.L. thanked the marshal again for his efforts and headed back to work. Thursday came and went, and Friday too. Swen paid J.L. more money that he thought he deserved.

J.L. thought a little shopping for Maddie and Jacob would be good before he headed out. He found some gingham material that Mrs. Rogers, the shopkeeper's wife, suggested. Maddie would enjoy making some nice things with it. And for Jacob a few sticks of candy and a kazoo that he and Maddie might later regret. He grabbed a couple more candy sticks for himself to enjoy on his ride out.

It was a fine afternoon and spring was moving right along. The trees, on the way, except for the oaks, were budding and even beginning to show new leaves. Everything seemed so green in the bright sun. There were hatches of flying insects that wanted to fly up his nose as he rode along. The birds seemed to be everywhere; the noisy calls of Red Winged Black Birds, Scrub Jays and Magpies mixed with the sounds of Chickadees, Mourning Dove and Quail. Geese and ducks were on the fly; their squawking making sure everyone knew they were there. Above the Chenoweth cliffs eagles and hawks soared, riding on the warm thermals of the afternoon. The concern that had been pestering J.L. about Jeffers disappeared as a morning mist would on the dawning of a hot dry day.

The people he met along the way all seemed as happy as he felt glad. He guessed that spring had sprung. Everyone smiled, waved and said "How do."

J.L. rode into his place just as the sun began to set low in the sky. In that arid country the warmth of the day was waning quickly and J.L. set about getting firewood in for the night. Jacob helped and then asked if he and his dad could shoot the bow and arrows at the target affixed to a straw bale. J.L. took time to tighten up the bow and show Jacob how to aim for a better shot. Maddie was busy inside but in a short while shouted out that supper was ready.

After grace everyone dug in, ready to enjoy a great meal at the end of the busy week. The talk was that of a happy family sharing the events of the week. They talked about the events of school, taking care of old Mr. Larson, work and such.

There was discussion about spring and the plans to get ready for it. Maddie and J.L. began to reminisce a bit, telling Jacob what it was like to come to this country nearly eight years before. They described how it was so much different than their home in Virginia and yet how they both fell in love with this place they decided to call home.

Jacob had a question on his mind, "Pop, I was over talking with Mr. Larson, remember all those arrowheads? He says there are probably plenty more. Do you think we could go up on those cliffs tomorrow and look for more of them?"

"We have a lot of work tomorrow, but if we get up early and get it done maybe your Ma will pack us some sandwiches and we'll go see what we can find in the afternoon."

Jacob was all excited and J.L. looked forward to it while Maddie treasured the thought of family together; at work and play.

"It's getting real late for me, where did the time go?" J.L. said, rising from the table.

"John, why don't you stay tonight?" You could sleep out in the parlor or take Jacob's bed tonight. After what you said about Jeffers I don't think I want you out on that road in the dark alone."

"I'll be alright," J.L. tried to assure but thinking that to not have to ride back to The Dalles would be a blessing.

"If you stay, then you can get an early start on all of that work and then on to your adventure upon the cliffs. I'd be happy to cook you a big breakfast," Maddie encouraged.

"I think I'd be a fool to turn down such an offer," J.L. smiled at both Maddie and Jacob.

The floor in front of the fire might not have been the most comfortable place to sleep but tonight, for J.L. it was a bit of heaven. He watched the fire for awhile, his sleepy eyes wanting to give in before he was quite ready to shut them. He also remembered what many other Friday nights had been about, drinking and whooping it up with other revelers. These folks all believing that the best way to shake off the dust of a long week was with beer, whiskey, gambling and cavorting.

In some way now it seemed foreign to him, but he concerned himself with what he would do if the urge to imbibe came back. For this evening he felt not only contentment, the quiet sounds of his family already a sleep and the crackling of the wood as it burned down. Once again, there was that peace that assured him that in some way, and somehow, things would all work out for the better. The last thing he remembered before the morning sun and the rooster crowing its fool head off was a little prayer, "Thanks Father God." For that night, the terrible dreams did not come.

Chapter Ten

This Day

"Boast not thyself of tomorrow; for thou knowest not what a day may bring forth."
Proverbs 27:1

Maddie was up before all of them, clanging dishes and pots and pans around in her way of being an alarm clock. She sang and not just to herself. J.L. had heard it many times before, "Shall we gather at the river, the beautiful, beautiful river." He knew it wasn't about the Columbia not so far from their home and it was a beauty too. No, this song was about a distant shore in a place where time was no more. Maddie wasn't pure of voice but she could carry a tune and what great talent she may not have had, she made up for in exuberance.

"Come on boys, the day is wasting. Get 'em up before I throw this wonderful breakfast of ham, and eggs, and taters, and biscuits to the coyotes," she said dragging out the words and ... ham ... and ... eggs, etc. etc.

J.L. went outside to wash in the washbasin on the porch. This morning, there was a hint of ice but spring was chasing the cold days away. The splash of cold water on his face and hands brought him alert in a second and he greeted the blue sky day with a 'Thank-you Lord' and thought no better day could be had.

After grace, while Jacob was about the serious business of eating as many scrambled eggs and chunks of ham as possible, between mouthfuls and coffee, Maddie and J.L. talked about what needed to be done.

"I've been making some good money and maybe we should get a few more head of cattle, maybe another horse, a good mare for breeding," J.L. said the excitement of the new day in his voice.

"I'm thinking we should grow some things and how about those orchard trees you promised me, way back," Maddie continued to prompt. "Remember that trip we made to Hood River and all those sweet apples, pears and cherries? If that isn't enough, think about all the pies and I could make you two."

"Pies!" Jacob chirped in.

"Maybe we could make a day of it next week; go over to Hood River and see about some trees," J.L. said, now determined to keep that old promise.

J.L. enjoyed the conversation and if it was trees Maddie wanted then he would get them for her. It was just a nice feeling to be like a family again and in fact some ways more of a family than he had ever felt before.

Everybody got busy after breakfast. There were animals to be fed, eggs to be gathered, bread to make, clothes to wash and mend.

J.L. and Jacob hitched up the plow to the two mules. Maddie had named them Jonah and Esau because of their obstinate nature, which they were happy to display that morning after having gone all winter without having to do an honest day's work. J.L. coaxed them with words, gestures and little bits of dried apples.

They set out in the far corner, back towards the cliffs, setting out to plow ten acres in the next week. J.L. would buy grass and grain seed in town. They were blessed with a wet spring that kept water available.

In the past J.L. dug channels to move water and keep the ground irrigated. The work this day was hard and pretty soon the sun began to feel very warm. Jacob stayed ahead of the mules throwing out rocks and big dirt clods. After a while, J.L. stopped to drink water from his old army canteen, which he shared with Jacob; along with some jerky and a candy stick he had on him. He peeled off his shirt, exposing a white chest to the sun. Jacob took a glance and looked shocked. J.L. had healed well, and most of the pain was gone, but the discoloration from all of the bruising was still very evident.

"It's alright, Son. I am fine but let this be a lesson to you, if you sow trouble, you will reap trouble," said J.L. as he poured water from his canteen on his neck and down the back of his shirt.

"What do you mean, Pop?" the boy asked with a look of puzzlement upon his face.

"Well, what are we out doing on this fine day?" J.L. asked his son.

"Plowing," Jacob answered matter of fact.

"And for what?" J.L. continued.

"Grass for them animals and some wheat and corn for us, so Momma can keep us in bread, corn-doggers and flapjacks," Jacob answered proud that knew so much.

"Well, what if we were out sowing thistles, brambles and poison oak seeds, what would we get?" J.L. asked again, using the advantage to make his point while putting his shirt back on.

"Uh, nothing but slivers, itching and trouble I guess, but why would any one want to do that?" said, Jacob, a look of puzzlement still on his young face.

"Nobody would or should. But maybe our lives are the same way. What we do and what we say is like sowing good or bad seed."

"So are you saying that those bruises are like a bad crop you got?" Jacob said, touching the now covered area on J.L.'s shirt.

"Exactly, that stupid drinking of mine and my mouth when I was drinking got me in to a tussle with some bad men who did this to me. Maybe they would have done it to somebody anyway. Maybe the one to blame for these bruises and the pain they caused is me." J.L. had thought about this a great deal while convalescing at Mrs. Valdez's. "That doesn't mean it was okay what they did but I have to be a holdin' to my own ways too. Trouble comes usually because you go looking or asking for it."

"So you're saying not to ever get in trouble?" Jacob asked, convinced that to not get into a little trouble now and then would be impossible.

"What I'm saying is, you have to take what's dished to you if you do get into trouble. Or as I heard it one time, if you want to dance you gotta pay the piper."

Jacob laughed at that, not really understanding but it set him off singing the song, "Skip, skip, skip to my Lou, my darling." And for the next hour they worked, Jacob, in the boundless energy of a ten year old boy, danced about while tossing rocks and clods while the mules and J.L. trudged along.

The noon hour came and Maddie called the men of her life in for dinner plus she had some sandwiches with beef and cheese made too for their big adventure.

After they had finished the meal Jacob said, "You could come to Momma!"

"I was thinking if I were invited I might. It has been a long time since I've been up on those cliffs. In fact, it was only once, when your father and I first came here. It was spring, I remember that. Is that fine with you, John?"

"We'd love to have the pleasure of your company that is if'in you can keep up," J.L. kidded. With that Maddie raced to the door, bounded out running like an antelope loping over the plains.

Jacob took off after her. J.L. grabbed the sandwiches, his canteen and followed after them at the quickest pace his sore body would go, which wasn't very fast or as graceful as an antelope. It was about a half mile to the edge of the cliffs. Then a steady back and forth as they climbed to the flat at the edge of the caves. They would stop now and then to take in the ever increasing view of the Columbia country, seeing more and more snow capped hills and mountains in both Washington and Oregon.

They climbed to the caves and rested in their shade. These caves were shallow and probably homes to man and animal alike over many centuries. With lighted matches, that burned out too quickly and burnt fingers, the three of them explored the caves. There was evidence of old fire pits. With a stick Jacob scratched around until he found a couple of arrow points in the dust.

J.L. wanted to go on top of the cliffs thinking that more points and other things of interest might be found. So the three of them traipsed and climbed the backside to the top.

Below they could see the Chenoweth Creek and the trees along its banks wearing a new dress of green.

From the top they were greeted with a view that seemed to show the whole of the gorge and the surrounding mountains gracing it. From where they were, Mt. Hood and Mt. Adams glittered like white pearls in the sun. They could also see Mt. St. Helens. They had heard tell that it once blew a bit of its top and some folks remembered it or heard tell of it from people who did. Now and then some trappers that still moved through the lands told how they had seen something like smoke coming from it.

To the south they could make out the tip of another mountain they thought was called Jefferson. To the North and barely visible on the horizon was a bit of white that could be Mt. Rainer.

Jacob had never seen such a scene before that he could remember. Maddie took the opportunity to quote a scripture she remembered from her lessons in Sunday school: ***"Thou crownest the year with goodness; and thy paths drop fatness. They drop upon the pastures of the wilderness: and the little hills rejoice on every side. The pastures are clothed with flocks; the valleys also are covered over with corn; they shout for joy, they also sing." Psalm 65:11-13"***

"What are you saying Momma?" Jacob asked.

"God made this for us and we can shout and praise His name," she said jubilantly. At that, this is exactly what she did, at the top of her lungs she shouted, "Praise be to God, Praise be to God!" over and over, and the sounded echoed across the way.

Soon Jacob started too and J.L. himself, bellowed like a cow stuck in the mud, "Praise be to God."

When they had finished and then only when their voices began to give out, Maddie said in a breathy whisper, "Watch through this year, Jacob, and see all that God provides." She gave him a smile of a knowing satisfaction in the Lord's ways for those who love Him.

They rested a bit and then the urge for more arrow heads sent the two boys, big and not so big, off again while Maddie rested in the shade of a willow. Now and then she would hear a whoop or a holler, "Pa, come quick" as her son and husband found another treasure.

They returned in a while, Jacob's hands and pockets full of ancient finds of a people and time now long ago. J.L. slumped to the ground, wiping sweat from his brow. He passed the canteen around and everyone took a long pull. Then out came the sandwiches which were devoured by J.L. and Jacob as if they had never eaten.

Jacob leaned up against his mother to tell of their finds but the warmth of the day and the fresh air soon brought them sleep. J.L., for a time rested against the tree too but after a while he walked out to the edge of the cliff, sat down and hung his legs over, leaned back against his outstretched arms, palms in the dirt.

It was so quiet he noted, some light wind blowing along the cliff edge, swallows swooping back and forth looking to take residence in the cliffs below. He closed his eyes, stretched out, conscience and subconscious flitting in and out as he began to doze.

Suddenly, in what seemed like just a moment later, he was jolted out of his reverie from the noise of a commotion behind him. He could hear Jacob screaming. He jumped to his feet, nearly losing his balance on the cliff edge. Gaining it back he spun to see Jacob in the clutches of none other than Clint Jeffers, looking mean as ever, dark, surly and shouting.

Maddie was trying to get to her feet, but Clinton, with a heavy boot to her chest, sent her reeling back to the ground, striking her head on the tree. She groaned, trying to get up but fell back as Clinton again pushed her with his boot.

"Stay down, woman, or the boy gets it!" Clinton shouted.

That is when J.L. noticed that Clinton held Jacob tight around his chest with his arm and bandaged hand. In the other hand he held a pistol, cocked, pointed and pressing against the boy's head. Maddie again started to rise to her feet determined to do something including sacrificing herself.

"You stay down, woman, or he gets hot lead!" the outlaw shouted.

Maddie had no choice but to do as he said. She sat there rubbing her head and trying to shake of the dizziness. By the time J.L. had started edging forward, wanting to get away from the cliff and as close to Jeffers so, if a chance would come, he could rush him. His plan was to hit him hard before any gunplay took place.

"You just stay where you are," shouted Jeffers, adding a few expletives. "In fact, you just move back to that edge and I'll tell you what we're all gonna do. You see my hand?" More expletives spat forth, "I'll never use it again. You ruint my gun hand and you are gonna pay. If you don't do as I say your son or that fine lookin' woman over there will pay in one way or another."

"What do you want, Jeffers, this is about you and me, not my family," J.L. said back to him trying to appear calm.

"Well, I will tell you what I want, but first you get on that edge as tight as you can."

J.L. did Clint's bidding, standing at the very edge, leaning somewhat backward to keep his balance.

"The Good Book says and eye for an eye and a tooth for a tooth, well you know what, that ain't good enough," Jeffers snarled. "No Sirree, I am going to exact my pound of flesh before your woman and kid and we are going to see if you soar like a bird or fall like a rock."

"What do you mean, Clint, what do you want? Let my boy go. What do you want from me to make up for your hand?" J.L. shouted back, hoping there was some way to reason with this mad dog of a man.

"I want to see you fly, or I want to see you fall, that is what I want," Jeffers shot back with a mean laugh. "Now you just flap those arms and jump. Jump I said!" There was an evil snicker in his voice and a braggart manner which said he loved his control of the situation.

J.L. looked down again, trying to calculate what might happen and how he might save himself. From where he stood, straight down, there was nothing but a hundred foot drop to the ground around the sloping cave entrance. He would surly break something if not everything. But to his left and down five to ten feet or so there was an outcropping of rock he might reach. Maybe he could land there and hold on. Maybe it would give him a moment to do something to save his family.

"Come on Matthews, what's it going to be, the boy with a bullet in his head or maybe this fine looking women or you over the edge?" Jeffers said waving the gun about.

"Wait, wait, I will jump but let me say goodbye to my family," J.L. implored.

"You go to hell, I'll say goodbye for you!" Jeffers shouted now pointing his pistol directly at J.L.

J.L. could see Maddie trying to struggle with something behind her. He needed to give her a moment if she was going to make an attack.

"You let the boy go and as soon as I see that I will jump, if I don't you can shoot me."

Clinton thought for a second and then let go of the boy and at that same time pulled on the trigger. J.L. jumped to his left, arms stretched out. The sound of the pistol echoed but by then he was over the edge. He hit the surface hard, the impact of it snatching away his breath. He grabbed at any rock and anything he could grab onto which didn't seem to be much and before he knew it he was sliding off down to the edge of the rocky outcrop.

J.L. tried hard to hold, his hands digging in until finally his fingers of his left hand caught in a rock that held him. He quickly searched with his other hand to find another hold, plus booted toes dug in too.

As he tried to save his life he did not hear two very solid thumps of heavy wood upon flesh that put Jeffers to the ground in a crumpled ball of meanness. Maddie hung over him for a second then banged him again on the head for good measure and then turned her attention to the cliff.

Jacob and Maddie quickly ran to the edge screaming, "John, Pa, Oh my God help us!" at the top of their voices. J.L. could pick up his head enough to see them off to his right, but he was unable to shout out because he was now trying to get his breath back. Maddie looked straight down and didn't see her husband lying a hundred feet below like expected.

'Where is he?' she thought in the second, thinking maybe he had rolled off the edge below into the brush so she couldn't see him. J.L. had gotten just enough breath back to let out a cry of an indistinguishable word but it was enough for Maddie and Jacob to hear and turn there attention to the left and to see J.L. hanging precariously on the little edge some ten feet below.

"Oh Lord please, hold on John!" Maddie yelled, dashing to a spot directly above him.

Jacob was there in a flash too and Maddie grabbed the boy before he got too close to the edge.

'What to do, what to do!', Maddie's mind raced. She had a four foot long, thick oak branch she had pummeled Jeffers with. She lay flat on her stomach and inched over the edge as far as she could.

"Jacob, hold my feet, sit down and dig in your heals for all your worth!" she shouted to her son who did immediately as she asked.

"John, can you reach me?" she shouted out.

Responding to her cry, J.L. slowly began to climb up the forty five degree angle of rock ledge. It was hard going even though he had just a short way to go. With every foot or two he climbed he slid back a foot, finding himself desperately grabbing whatever he could to hold on to. But as he got closer to the cliff edge he was able to grab a hold of a bush that had rooted itself there and seemed to be sturdy enough to hold some of his weight. However, at the edge he could not reach the stick Maddie extended as far as her arms would go.

He would have to try to stand. So slowly, hand grasping at the rock cliff, he edged himself up onto his knees and then slowly to a standing position like a trapeze artist on a slim line. Rocks and dirt sliding under his feet and falling from the cliff edge to below were making it hard for him to stand, keep a balance and not fall.

From there he was able to grab the thick stick with one hand and the other hand grabbing and pulling at the rock along the edge, feet dug in and what seemed like an eternity of time. Finally Maddie was able to grab him by his shirt collar and literally drag the big man, him kicking at the rock, up and over the edge. They all laid there for a moment catching their breath.

On J.L.'s mind in that moment was a marveling of how strong his wife was when push came to shove. And what about Jeffers, were they still in danger?

In gasps of air he tried to talk about the latter, "What . . . did you do, did . . . you thump him? Is he dead?"

"I don't know." said Maddie, now sitting up and grabbing Jacob to cradle him.

"Are you alright, honey?" she asked.

"Yeah, Mom, I'm okay." But Jacob's eyes were the size of saucers and his complexion the color of milk that you might put in those saucers and he was shaking as if it was a cold winter's day.

"I hit him as hard as I could," said Maddie.

J.L. was now on his feet, but crouching. He wanted to do something to make sure that Jeffers was out of commission and that they could get to the marshal as quickly as possible.

"You two stay and lay low, make a poor target for him to shoot."

The two lay back down, but both were turned to look towards the oak tree where Maddie had hit Jeffers. J.L. approached the area some hundred feet from the edge, gingerly and staying low. But he didn't see a thing. There was no body lying close to the tree although, as he arrived, he could see the outline in the spring grass where someone had laid and there was some blood on the grass.

He bent over to see more closely when, all of a sudden, a shot rang out from some distance. Then there was the sound of ricochet as the bullet hit rock, not more than two feet from him. J.L. hit the ground, as another shot buzzed by, this time on the other side of him, striking the tree, bark exploding into the air. J.L. waited for a third shot but all was quiet. He waited for a full minute continuing to look towards the direction the shots had been fired. He got to his knees and, in the distance, saw some dust rise and the sound of horse hooves hammering on the ground. The sound grew fainter and Clint Jeffers, he thought, rode off to plan attack for another day.

"John, John, are you alright?" Maddie called out.

He hollered right back, "Yes, I am fine, come on let's get down from here."

The three of them took off half running and crouching, half carrying Jacob until they got down the hill and could disappear in the brush and trees that hugged the banks of the Chenoweth stream. They followed it down until they arrived at their cabin close to its' banks. Upon entering the cabin J.L. went for his carbine on the wall, loaded it while thinking about what to do next. He knew that he needed to get to the marshal but he was not willing to leave his family alone. What he really wanted to do was mount up and take off after Clinton, thinking maybe he might be able to trail him and catch him. Jeffers probably didn't have any more than a half hour lead on him.

He was now bothered that Jeffers had tracked him to his home. Evidently he had been spying on them for sometime and followed them up the cliffs to carry out his dastardly plan. He was beginning to fully grasp that Jeffers was not going to let this go anytime soon or probably ever. Now he also knew that this villain would harm his family as well.

Maddie was watching her husband thinking and pondering, his brow furrowed like a freshly plowed field.

"John, get to the marshal! Maybe he will form a posse now and go after hi,." she jumped in.

"What about you two?"

"We will go over and stay with Mr. Larson. His place is like a fortress and he has armament in there, we will be protected. If Jeffers knows you are on his tail he won't be coming this way." Now her voice rose, "But don't do this by yourself," she warned.

"I want to be sure you will be safe."

"John, go and go fast," said Maddie, literally pushing him out the door.

* * *

J.L. was glad to find the marshal in on this Saturday afternoon. He quickly, but in detail, told him what took place upon the cliffs. The marshal responded quickly, especially when J.L. told of the threat to Maddie and Jacob. He had a soft spot for them and he wasn't willing for this situation to go any further. In a matter of minutes he sent his two deputies to bring on recruits and trackers. Meanwhile he and J.L. headed for the back side of the Chenoweth cliffs with the understanding that everyone would meet there as soon as possible.

The two snooped around the hills and trees leading to the edge of the cliffs. They found sign where Jeffers had left his horse tied while he mounted the hill and his attack. There was some blood at the sight indicating that in the blows that Maddie had delivered to the back of Jeffers, one of them drew blood, likely from his head.

By Three P.M. the deputies had brought four other men with them plus a tracker who had a few hounds used for hunting bear and mountain lion. The blood helped the dogs to get a scent and soon they were leading the way on the bloody heals of Jeffers.

They came to another creek, Mills Creek by name. Here the dogs lost the scent for a bit. But one of the deputies and J.L. followed the creek down, rather than up, and came across fresh hoof prints. They hollered out and the tracker and dogs came along. Soon the dogs were barking and carrying on, fresh on the trail again. This in turn now put the marshal and J.L. in front with the tracker close behind and the rest of them not far behind. There was a sense by all that it would be only minutes before they were on their quarry and the hope was that that the light of day would hold out, but the shadows were growing long.

Jeffers tracks showed that he was making a long arc, now leading back towards The Dalles, high up on a ridge, riddled with great rocks, oak and brush.

"Boys," the marshal hollered out "hold up a minute, he has got to be up among these rocks waiting, maybe to ambush some of us as soon as he gets a shot."

The trapper sought to gain control of his dogs, but they were not to be stopped, beast or man, they were close and would not be held back.

The posse gathered close but did not dismount. The trapper went on ahead but still some ways behind the dogs, rifle cocked and raised. Others started pulling pistols and rifles from holsters and scabbards.

The sudden explosion of powder and primer told them they were correct. From an outcropping not more than one hundred yards up and away Jeffers unleashed lead. One shot hit one of the dogs, who let out a sorrowful yelp and crumpled to the ground.

Another shot kicked dust not more than a foot from the trapper's boots. He, in turn, leapt back and hit the ground trying to become a small target.

The sun's glare was against the posse as it began to set in the west on that terrible day. The rock outcropping stood dark against the setting sun and no one could tell where on that rock the shots where fired.

With heads down and crouching, the men of the posse where off there horses and scattered behind the nearest rocks or trees that they could find. The trapper's other hound stayed close to his fallen brother and howled but would not move. The marshal thought to shout out to Jeffers encouraging him to give up, but on second thought realized that would not happen. For this moment the bad man had the advantage.

Jeffers, however, decided to make his thoughts heard and shouted out behind a rock. "You boys, just hold back! I can take that other dog and the trapper right now, and a couple of you who think you are hidden are nothing but sittin' ducks!"

Everybody scrunched down harder but Jeffers fired off another shot to prove his point, this one coming with in a few feet of the marshal.

"You see what I mean; now I don't want to shoot any of you. My beef is not with you but with Matthews. Let him and I finish this out here and now!" Jeffers shouted again.

"No way," the marshal retorted, "you will get your day in court and you can say your piece there, but before this day is through, you will either be in jail or your carcass will be at the undertakers."

The marshal looked around to see where every one was placed but didn't see Matthews at the spot he had been a moment ago. Now off to the left and up, in the shadows of a gulch he could he could see him creeping to the base of the rocks. He thought that maybe J.L. had a sense about where Jeffers might be in those rocks. He did not want J.L. to take this task on his own but by now he didn't have a lot of say in the matter.

The marshal thought quick and whispered out to the posse, "J.L. is in that gulch, at my count, you shoot enough lead into that rock above him to keep Jeffers hunkered down."

They all understood that this was to be a diversion to let J.L. get a chance at Jeffers. At the count of three their guns began to blaze. J.L., at first, ducked down wondering if he had put him self in harm's way. He looked back and saw the marshal waving at him and gesturing him on. In this moment that the lead flew with fury J.L. was able to get up and behind the rock. On this side sunlight lit everything and he could see Jeffers not ten feet away, cowered like the dog that he was.

J.L.'s first thought was to shoot him where he squatted but then the gunplay ceased and Jeffers was moving to stand and shoot from his vantage point. J.L. jumped to his feet and leapt the space between the two, his body flying, arms in front of him, ready to block and hit. He smashed into the back of Jeffers with the full force of his two hundred plus pounds. Jeffers face and front hit up against the rocks but he tried to turn and swat at J.L. with his bandaged hand, and with the other hand, trying to get his pistol for a close shot.

Jeffers, however, was at a disadvantage and J.L. bounced him again against the rocks, this time Jeffers gun went flying from his only usable hand. The next blow to body, against rock, crumpled Jeffers and knocked him unconscious.

J.L. shouted out, "I've got him, he's down and you all can come up."

The men came running. The trapper, who was the closest came in first, yelling and swearing, trying to get a good kick at the still prostrate Jeffers until J.L. grabbed him around the waist and moved him back.

"You son of a . . . you done kilt my best dog and my best friend! I hope you hang and if you don't, so help me, you'll be feed for the other dogs." The trapper spat, trying again to get a kick in at the still unconscious bad man.

The marshal was next along with the deputies. They soon had Jeffers handcuffed and, for good measure, his feet bound too. Then they decided to see if he still was alive and checked for pulse and breath. He was a pretty beat up hombre. There was the gash on the back of his head from where Maddie had pelted him and a bloodied nose and a gashed forehead where J.L. had bounced him off the rocks twice. Jeffers was far from dead and as he came to murderous words spewed from his mouth.

* * *

Now back in town and at the jail, Jeffers was a sight. He had been banged around so much that day that the marshal sent for the Doc to stitch and patch him up. The doctor also checked Jeffers hand which was healing poorly and would probably never be of much use again. He had been out hiding so long that the smell of him was more than the little office and jail could bear so he was taken over for a scrubbing at the local bath house. When he returned he was shaven and clean but the look of hatred and scorn on his face would not wash off.

"You will get a fair trial, Clint Jeffers, mark my word," said the marshal. "I will make sure of that, but I will also make sure that if I have a word in it, you will get some fair time to think about your ways in the state pen," he added, glaring at the sullen man in the cell.

The marshal, however, was not done with his speech as he paced back and forth in front of the barred cell. "You have been a thorn in my side for a long time and now you have crossed the line. Maybe it's time for you to think about how your outlaw ways have gotten you nothing but trouble. Your pards are dead and I think you bear some of that responsibility. You killed that poor dog. You threatened a little boy with a gun to his head and his mamma as well along with all this stuff with Mathews. Enough is enough! You are not going anywhere soon so you can sit and sulk or you can think about what got you to these bad ways that will cost you a lot of freedom!"

Jeffers, by his silence, chose to sit and sulk. Already in his mind was the question, 'how do I get out of here?'

* * *

J.L. was exhausted when he got home to Maddie and Jacob. Too hungry to eat, he just slouched in the old leather chair near the fire Maddie had stirred up. A hearty bowl of stew sat on the table next to him untouched but he did sip at the coffee. Soon Maddie brought a wash basin full of warm water, soap and some salve.

"You are looking a little rough for the range. Let's see what damage the day has done." said Maddie trying to comfort and lighten the mood.

She unbuttoned his shirt and peeled it and was amazed at how many new cuts and scratches he had on his chest from the fall to the rock on the cliff and the fight with Clinton. She, tenderly as she could, washed and applied salve to his arms, shoulders, chest and stomach.

"It's alright; I am just ready for a good night's sleep. How about your head Maddie, you alright?" He asked, reaching his hand out to touch the back of Maddie's auburn head.

"Just a little bump." she said, rubbing the tender spot, with J.L.'s hand atop hers. "Sleep in the bed tonight. I don't mind staying out here by the fire."

Tonight he wasn't going to argue, even the gentlemen that he was trying to be. Soon he was tucked between sheets and blankets and he marveled how long it had been since he had slept here. It felt good and he could feel sleep coming quickly. At the same time and for the first time in weeks, he wished for a long pull on a whiskey bottle, thinking how it might ease the pain. The thought then worried him and he pushed it away reminding himself of all the trouble it brought, including why he was so beat to a pulp again and his family having been in harm's way on this day.

Maddie sat beside him, her hand on his forehead and she began to talk, but not to him. "Lord, I thank thee for thy protection today. Thou watched out for us today and kept us safe and for that we are grateful. I thank Thee Lord that you saw fit to help us today and preserve our lives but also apprehend Mr. Jeffers. I thank Thee Lord for our good marshal and his fine men who put their lives at stake for us today. I thank Thee for old Fred the trapper; please comfort him tonight in the loss of his beloved dog. I pray too for Mr. Jeffers, may he see the error of his ways. And Lord God I thank Thee for my husband who is a man that is brave and strong and I ask that you heal him and give him rest. I thank thee, Lord, for your providence and mercy to us and it is in the name of Your Son that I pray."

And with that, and a kiss on the forehead, J.L. was left in the dark room to sleep. For a moment he considered what good tomorrow could bring with Jeffers now locked up and out of his and his family's life for a good long while he hoped.

Chapter Eleven

Good Tidings

"Heaviness in the heart of a man, maketh it stoop;
But a good word maketh it glad."
Proverbs 12:25

The day dawned bright. As J.L. awakened he could hear Maddie out in the kitchen busy with the clank and clang of pans. She was singing a hymn about bringing in the sheaves. He realized that today was Sunday. It didn't seem so because of the horror of yesterday.

He moved gingerly from the bed but was surprised to discover that he felt better than he thought he would. Maddie was already dressed for Sunday in a dark blue dress. Jacob was at the table having his breakfast, long towel tucked into his Sunday best shirt so there would be no chance that bacon grease or preserves would assault it.

"Are you hungry? Breakfast is waiting," called Maddie.

"Yeah, Pop, are you alright? You should be hungry as an ole bear," Jacob added.

"I am," stated J.L. and then added a growl to confirm to Jacob that he was while brushing Jacob's hair with his paw of a hand.

"How do you feel this morning?" Maddie asked.

"Not too bad for a man who jumped off a cliff. Are you two alright this morning? That turned out to be a terrible day and we didn't get to talk it out." J.L. said as he approached Maddie, pecking her on the cheek.

"I am fine Pop, but I wanna to know what happened," Jacob stated.

"I promise, Jacob, we will find some time for that today," answered J.L., knowing that sooner the better. He could imagine how a boy could have many questions and concerns about such a thing.

"John, I don't know how well you feel," Maddie started to approach him that this was Sunday and there was church to attend, "but Jacob and I need to leave pretty quick."

"Not with out me your not," J.L. said to dispel her concern.

"Oh good, they have a guest preacher at the church today, a gentlemen that comes from across the river to speak to us this morning. The place will be full. There will be a potluck picnic after. I already have chicken and biscuits ready to go," stated Maddie in one long flow and as a convincer to why it would be good for her husband to attend.

"What time did you get up this morning or was it last night, to do all this?" J.L. asked, while wolfing down his breakfast. He was always amazed at her energy.

"No, I did it after you were in bed. I was restless and you two were sawing such logs, a woman couldn't have slept if she'd wanted."

J.L. finished up quick, found some clothes he hadn't worn in some while. Then he hooked up the buck board and soon the family was on their way the few miles to the Methodist church in The Dalles. Along the way, Maddie was quiet, apparently, as J.L. thought, just enjoying the beautiful day and maybe thinking about yesterday. That was all Jacob wanted to talk about incessantly. He thought maybe it's just the little boy's way of coming to terms with it.

Maddie, in her meditation, however, was far from the events of yesterday; she was praying mightily. She knew that the guest preacher that came today with the intent of preaching a sermon that would convince the lost to become saved. So she prayed, for her husband that today might be his day of salvation.

As Maddie predicted the church lot was packed. J.L. found a place towards the back of the church to pull in the wagon. By the back of the door of the church J.L. noticed, lay a big dog, asleep. He was black and wooly like a bear. For some reason the dog seemed familiar but he did not know why.

Other families were arriving in wagons, on horse back and on foot. Many greeted the Matthews family with pleasantries and it was of a comfort to both J.L. and Maddie. Marshal James and his wife were also at the church; they all greeted each other and he and his wife asked about how the family was faring. Mrs. James gave Maddie, Jacob and even J.L. a big hug and told them she was praying around the clock for them.

J.L. felt uncomfortable inside the church, especially with all those people, but it felt good to be there. He took comfort in the old hymns, familiar to him from his days as a boy in Virginia. He listened to the prayers from the pastor and felt a little embarrassed when he included his family in the prayers. Finally the pastor introduced the guest speaker. Pastor Gideon Thomas was his name. He was tall, angular, dressed in black and J.L. thought as old as the hills that were around The Dalles.

The old man stood erect, smiled a big smile and thanked the pastor for having him and greeted those gathered in the name of the Lord. He was a commanding presence, comfortable on the platform, and, J.L. thought, probably been preaching since Noah docked the Ark. And again, like the dog out back, there was an air of familiarity about the man that he could not put his finger on. He could not imagine how he might know him.

"Today, our lesson comes from the Prophet Isaiah, from the sixty-first chapter, commencing at verse one," the old preacher began: "'***The Spirit of the Lord God is upon me; because the Lord hath anointed me to preach good tidings unto the meek; he hath sent me to bind up the broken hearted, to proclaim liberty to the captives, and the opening of the prison to them that are bound; to proclaim the acceptable year of the Lord, and the day of vengeance of our God; to comfort all that mourn.***'"

"I came to this great and wild land nearly 40 years ago, so moved was I about the massacre of my great mentor Marcus Whitman, family and associates in the Lord's ministry. My hope was, in someway, to help fill his shoes. Not that only one person could do such a thing. I considered that, perhaps, the Good Lord would see fit to give me opportunity among the natives and the new settlers to tell of a greater land that rests beyond the blue of this sphere and awaits the faithful.

And now, for this nearly forty years, I have traveled these lands of Oregon, Washington and farther to preach the Good News of our Lord and Savior Jesus Christ. That "Good News" message has been the same message that has been preached for nigh on to two millennia by a near endless band of brothers and sisters imparting nothing other than the central and saving message, ***"For God so loved the world that He gave His only begotten Son, that whosoever believeth in him should not perish, but have everlasting life."***

And the mission to speak is always to tell who makes this great offer. It is that perfect God and that perfect man, in the being of Jesus Christ, who walked and remains among us though the Holy Ghost. It is He that would seek unholy man and desire to save him from his sin and from himself."

He went on, "I have found both glory and heartache in this land. I have traveled through places so spectacular and yet so barren of folk one would wonder if God didn't make these places just for himself, sharing it only with the beasts that inhabit them. I have met all kinds of people along the way. Mostly good people but of independent stock, bound and determined to make a life for themselves regardless of the pestilence that stalks and kills, the winter winds that whip, the dry hot days that parch a man so that he can hardly move or think.

I have talked with every hue of a person, from every nation, it seems, bound by the mystique of the Oregon Trail and what lies beyond. All seek a New Jerusalem, a bit of Heaven, Eden but east of the Cascades, Shangri-La, Paradise and any other dream of a place of milk and honey that one could not hope to be happier in.

I have also noted that these perfect places seem to exist in one's mind and one's mind only. That paradise here, as grand as this Oregon country is, is also fraught with struggle, loss, heartache and pain. Many have thought, 'It would be paradise if only my beloved wife and not died of the pox, if my sweet child was not taken by the influenza, if my stock had not taken ill or had been carried off by wolf and lion, if the frost hadn't killed the crops or the fire hadn't burnt my home'. I have heard this from nearly all. It seems like paradise is at the door but it seems to enter with complaint and sorrow as well.

And he continued with "Well, I tell ye, brothers and sisters, happiness comes and goes on this mortal plain. Today you may know happiness and even some pleasure and yet on the morrow pain and grief pound loudly upon your door. But I have come not to tell you of happiness but of joy; unspeakable joy.

I bring you ***good tidings*** in that you can be born again and born for a new life here and a new there," continued the old preacher, his arms and hands gesturing at every phrase.

"I bring you this good news to let you know that your hearts need not be troubled. That there is a great God and King who will seek to ***bind up the broken hearted.*** Even in their sadness and grief that joy still is there to see them through no matter how gloomy the night or bright, with promise, the day.

I bring you good news to inform you that He hath set a day ***to proclaim liberty to the captives*** of sin. It is this snare that entangles through immorality, debauchery and evil. Ye not be bound by it anymore, for those who take of the spirits that lead to hell, ye can be free and free indeed from them.

I bring you good news ***to proclaim the acceptable year of the Lord,*** and that is today, this very day. God accepts, loves and forgives you your many sins. Repent and know that to not receive this will separate you from the love that the Father, through His Son, has for you.

I also warn you ***the day of vengeance of our God*** is here for those who are proud, wicked, immoral and unrepentant.

I give you great news for today. At this very moment God Almighty comes ***to comfort all that mourn.***"

For some time the old preacher exhorted, pleaded and, at times, seemed to threaten hell itself on the packed room. All that were in the room, and it was considerable, including many who stood in the back and the sides, were rapt upon the speaker. Occasionally someone would shout "Amen". Like Maddie, in that hall, many prayed for those who had been encouraged and cajoled to attend this special day. Finally, with perspiration beading on his forehead and a quiver in his voice, this servant of God invited those who had never found the Lord, or had fallen away, to come forward, have hands laid upon them and be prayed for them. The choir, on cue, sang "Amazing Grace".

Many on that fine day came forward. There was weeping of sadness and tears of joy by those who found their way to the Savior. J.L. fidgeted, shook and wanted to stand and go forward too. There was another part of him that wanted to just go and get out. It was hard for him to be around so many people. He didn't know why because this is not how it had always been. Maddie could see that J.L. was struggling. She placed her hand around his big hand, "John, I love you and God loves you."

The family stayed for the picnic and social afterwards. Many had heard about the terrible to-do with Jeffers the day before and wanted to know if all was alright with them. As the social began to finish and people started leaving, Jacob asked if he could stay with some friends in town. They would make sure he got to school in the morning. Maddie and J.L. agreed.

On the way home Maddie talked brightly of the days events. 'She surely loved that church and it's people,' J.L. said to himself. He could begin to understand why this was such a lifeline for her and Jacob, especially over these last months and years. He realized too, that he had just not been there much for the two of them.

J.L. waited for his opportunity, "Maddie, I want you to know that I wanted to go up there with the rest of them today. But, it was like I was frozen, like a scared cat frozen in his tracks." He felt embarrassed to say such a thing.

"It's alright, John, I think I knew that," Maddie quietly reassured, putting her hand on her husband's arm.

"I don't know what it is, I get around all of those people and I want to run or hide and for no good reason," J.L. tried to explain, though this discussion had come up before.

"I think it had to do with that terrible war, all that happened to you," Maddie comforted.

"But that was a long time ago now," J.L.'s voice trailed off.

"I probably don't know much about what I'm talking about but I think some things just take more time that we think they ought to so we can come to peace with them," Maddie continued to assure.

"Well, I want you to know, that even though I didn't go up there, I was there in my mind and spirit. And when that old preacher, who I thought might bring hell down on us there for a time, anyway, what I want to say is when he made the invite and prayed the sinner's prayer, I prayed it as my own too," J.L. said stammering, but determined, that Maddie know that he had accepted the Lord that morning.

Maddie hugged her husband and tears were in her eyes. "That is the best good news you could ever tell me!"

And on this fine day, as they rode out of The Dalles, past all the saloons, clubs and even the grand Umatilla House, the desire to stop and drink was the farthest thing from J.L.'s mind.

* * *

The next morning came with some rain and wind to remind them that winter didn't always give up early in the Oregon country. J.L. and Maddie had done something they hadn't done for many, many months. They shared their old bed together, entwined, lost in a new sense of love for each other and for God. Maddie thought to herself, maybe this is part of what holy matrimony is about.

She sang sweetly as she fixed breakfast for the two of them. J.L. shaved and washed up and donned work clothes. His plan was to work that day at the Blacksmith's shop and then pick up Jacob and the two of them would ride home on Gus. He would pay a visit to the marshal's office as requested; swear out a statement of all that occurred.

Maddie packed up a noon meal that would feed a small army, gave her husband a big kiss and tried to squeeze the life out of him, not so quick to want to let him go. J.L. squeezed back, lifted Maddie a foot or two off the ground swinging her around and plopping her in the old rocker on the front porch. They laughed, Maddie swung open handed at J.L.'s backside as he climbed on Gus.

"You are a sight Maddie, and I can hardly wait for the end of day, to see you in the sunset, looking sweeter than any thing around this great country could ever look," J.L. complimented, grinning from ear to ear.

* * *

"Vell, good morning! That is quite a smile you are a 'verring tis morning," said Swen.

J.L. told him about the weekend but smiled most when he told him that Maddie and he had patched things up. The two men were busy past noon before they got a break for a noon meal. As the two of them were eating, trying their best to consume all that Maddie had packed and talking about Jeffers, a man came in that Swen knew.

"Vell, if it isn't Brawdie Johnson*. Vhat are you doing up in these parts?" Swen asked the burly man who entered the shop.

"I had some business in Portland and I stayed at the Umatilla last night and now I'm getting ready to head out tomorrow back down south. But it's good to see you, Swen!" said Brawdie extending a paw of a hand.

"J.L. tis be Brawdie, von of the best blackies around, next to me. Now he is like a town mayor or something, vhat do you have going down in the center part of our state? You seem to be a building a town. Vhat did you decide for the name of that place?"

After shaking Sven's hand he extended his hand to J.L. who shook it generously.

*Brawdie Johnson was a real blacksmith and accredited with starting the town of Mitchell

"I never named a town before but it's called Mitchell, after the senator. And this place is busting at the seams. We've got quite a few people coming in there. We got a nice valley, good water for the desert and, well, it just seems a nice place that others want to be in. Stores are planned and a school is already built and it'll be interesting to see which comes first the saloons or a church," Bawdie said in one long thought and with a growing excitement in his voice.

"So you have some business here too? You a plannin' on stayin' another night?" Swen asked.

"Yeah, I am thinking maybe I should see about buying a herd of cattle to feed to all those folk coming in there, get some ranches started. I was hoping to talk with someone up here," Brawdie answered.

"Hey, J.L. vhat about that outfit you worked for, think they might be interested?" Swen asked.

"I could ride out there and see. It's getting late in the day and I need to get Jacob from school," J.L. answered, thinking it would be good to see them all at the ranch and this might be a good opportunity.

"Well, that's alright to wait to tomorrow," Brawdie interjected. "I still have some business here in town. Maybe we could ride out in the morning, if ole Swen will stop breaking your back for a bit."

They made plans for the next day and Brawdie and Swen made plans for supper after the work day and then departed.

J.L. was glad for this opportunity. It would be good for him to ride out and talk to his old boss. He had felt the need for some time. He wanted Noah High to know that he had turned over a new leaf.

"I bettcha Brawdie will want cattle right away, probably pay your boss for em on the spot," Swen said interrupting J.L.'s thoughts.

"He will need to have someone drive them down," J.L. thought out loud.

"I've been a little worried about vhat I can do for you. Work that has been piled up is about done and things will probably get quiet for a spell." Swen added, "maybe you might see if you and some of his boys could drive those cattle down to . . . what he say the name of that place . . . oh yeah, Mitchell."

J.L. loved the open range and the thought of seeing someplace new was exciting. He always knew he had a bit of wanderlust in him. He didn't want to leave Maddie and Jacob behind with things so new but he would need the work too.

J.L. finished up for the day, making it a little early, so that he could get to the marshal's office. When he arrived the marshal was there working on paper work and looking disgruntled in the process.

"Come on in, J.L., I am just finishing up some reports. This writing drives me up the wall but it is important to do. I'd rather be chasing after the likes of Jeffers all over creation than sitting stuck to this desk."

J.L. and the marshal spent a half hour together going over the events of the attack. The marshal grunted in disgust at how Jeffers had manhandled Jacob but laughed at the thought of Maddie whooping up on Jeffers with a big stick.

"I shouldn't laugh but he is such a scoundrel, he had it coming, I guess," said the marshal.

"What do you think will happen now?" asked J.L. thinking about the possibility of the cattle drive and Maddie and Jacob's safety.

"He is not going anywhere soon, 'cept over to state prison probably. The judge will be here next week and then we can convene a court. It is hard to imagine that he won't get a few years behind those bars for his ways. He has been a pain in this community's hind end for a long time. It's hard to imagine that a jury of his peers won't want to put him away for as long as the law allows."

J.L. told the marshal the possibility of the cattle drive that could last a few weeks. The marshal reassured J.L. that everything would be done to keep Jeffers locked up tight.

"His two running mates being dead, I don't know if there is anyone else around that would be so keen on getting this bad fella out, at least with out risking being locked up themselves," the marshal reassured. "I think your troubles with this fella will be behind you for some time. The welcome mat will never be out for him here again, if I have any say so. When he does get out in a few years, we will show him the door out."

The marshal then changed the subject and asked, "So what did you think of that preacher yesterday?"

J.L. took a moment before answering. "He had a lot to say that got me thinking, my life, the liquor and all as been on my mind for some time. I guess his words, or the good Lord's words that he spoke, really helped to convince me that it is time to turn things around."

"So you made a commitment then?" the marshal asked.

"Yes Sir, I have, I have had enough of that. I don't know why I did it in the first place. Some how for me the war and all that it was about and the liquor, well, I don't know, it just gets confusing at times. But I think I have found my answer and it is this Jesus and, somehow in someway, He will work it all out if I just let Him," J.L. said with some emotion showing in his face and voice.

"I am very glad to hear that! You are a likable fella and I think you have great potential and it will be nice to have you on this side with us, rather than the other," the marshal exclaimed.

"One thing that I can't figure out is why that old man seemed familiar. Does he have a big black dog do you know?"

"Oh, you saw Goliath waiting out back of the church did you?" The marshal asked. "He is a great dog, faithful to his master and goes everywhere with him. Did that dog seem familiar to you too?"

"Yeah, now that you mention it. Why do you ask?" J.L. was puzzled.

"Because it was Goliath that found you with your head stuck in the creek. It is the preacher, that circuit rider, who pulled you out of there and took you to Mrs. Valdez."

"He's the one!" J.L. said incredulously. He felt overwhelmed to realize that the same man that spoke of the Lord's salvation was also the one who saved him from certain death.

"He is the Good Samaritan that saved you and paid Mrs. Valdez to look after you," the marshal said in a quiet almost reverent voice.

"I wished I had known that yesterday, I would of thanked him," J.L. said with a disappointment in his voice but at least glad to know.

"I was going to try to introduce the two of you yesterday, but with so many people and then duty called so I didn't get a chance."

"I wonder if he is still in town, I want to say thanks."

"No," the marshal said, shaking his head, "He left this morning on the Lord's business east and south. You know, he travels many a mile to share the gospel. He will be back through, and I would imagine the parson would know how you might get in touch with him."

"Thanks marshal, I appreciate all you have done and thanks for letting me know," J.L. said while pummeling the marshal's hand in his.

* * *

J.L. picked up Jacob and they headed for home riding on Gus. A rain shower had come and gone leaving a brilliant sunny day like was often the case in the high desert country at spring's onset. The flora of the Columbia River was fragrant and shimmered as they proceeded out of town. Jacob filled J.L. in on his day at school. J.L. decided to wait to tell about the preacher when they were all gathered around the supper table tonight.

As the two of them rode into the ranch nestled on the banks of the Chenoweth stream, the trees along the edge looked ready to burst in celebration of spring. Maddie could be seen taking clothes down from the clothesline. J.L. took a moment just to admire her beauty and carriage. She stood straight and tall, wispy almost, but strong too. He thought, in his mind, the rough years had been kind to her. In his mind she didn't look a lot different from her early days. He felt blessed to have her for his wife and to have her again when she sure had no good reason to put up with him.

He couldn't help but holler out, "Hello, you beautiful gal, you."

Jacob giggled and he thought it looked like Maddie blushed.

"Hello my boys!" she shouted out turning from the task. "How was your day? Are you hungry because I have a beef steak and taters cooking."

Maddie's boys washed up and soon they were gathered together, holding hands, eyes closed and heads bowed. There was silence for a minute as everybody waited for Maddie to pray, which had pretty much been the custom. However, Maddie waited, hoping her man would get the hint.

J.L. did feeling uneasy and a little tongue tied but he prayed anyway. "Well, Lord, here we are again, and we thank you for the day you have given us, the rain and the place we call home. We, uh, thank you for the cattle on the hills and the spuds in the fields."

Jacob started to giggle but Maddie kicked him lightly under the table.

"Well, Lord, I guess all I can say is just thanks and thanks a lot, and uh, Amen."

J.L. was embarrassed a little but glad he did it.

The three of them tore into dinner eating everything that was there including some tender greens that had survived winter and sprung up in the garden.

J.L. could hardly wait to tell Maddie all the news and started before finishing his first bite. She, in turn, was grateful to God and counted it a miracle when she learned about the preacher being the one that had found her husband. She was less excited about the cattle drive possibility but felt that it was probably best and the money would help. There was still much to do this spring and it would take some money. After Jacob had finished and went to play, and gather some firewood, Maddie and J.L. stayed at the table, finishing the coffee.

"If this drive happens, how long do you think you would be gone?" Maddie asked.

"Probably two weeks, maybe three," J.L. answered, then added, "I won't go if you don't want me to."

"I don't want you to go, perhaps this would be best and I am sure it will be alright," Maddie tried to assure herself.

"Maddie, I'm a different man now. I will just do the work and there will be no trouble from me, I promise. Isn't much around there anyway but sage brush, I suspect. I can make us some money and I can prove to myself, being around those other cowpokes, that I can resist the devil. I know I can do this."

"If you say so, then, you go with my blessings but you better be home in three weeks or I'll come looking for you."

* * *

The next morning J.L. met Brawdie at the Umatilla House. He entered through the plush lobby and marveled that such a fancy place was here in The Dalles. The great lobby was busy with men and women coming and going. There was every kind of person from finely dressed ladies, garish dressed gamblers to ranchers and farmers traveling to and from other places in Washington and Oregon. Brawdie was at the front desk settling up with the clerk.

"Good morning, J.L., I am ready to head out to that ranch. Do you think your old boss will be open to selling me cattle? I hope he can give me a good price because that is a ways to drive 'em," Brawdie greeted and asked.

"Mr. High is a fair and honorable man, Brawdie, I believe he will try to do his best for you," J.L. stated.

The two men left the hotel, Brawdie retrieved his horse from the livery and the two rode off together. On the way both shared bits about their lives as they rode the five miles up on the plateau.

Soon the Flying High came into view, perched above the town and the river. From there J.L. could see Mt. Adams to the North and even make out a little of Mt. Rainer which seemed smaller in the distance than what he had been told.

Noah High was there, busy with the other ranch hands in branding and marking. He took the moment to meet with J.L. and Brawdie and was most cordial with both of the men. After some negotiations a deal was struck for a hundred head of cattle.

J.L. had just a minute to talk with his old boss. It was a busy day on the ranch and Jonah seemed to have a lot of other irons in the fire on that day too. He did tell him quickly of his new ways and ask for the job driving the cattle. Brawdie explained how to get to Mitchell and showed them on a map. A date was set for departure and Brawdie headed out, back to home. Jonah was obviously a forgiving man and was quick to agree to J.L. joining the others on the drive. J.L. shook Jonah's hand so hard one would have thought watching, that it might have came off in the process.

* * *

"We've set a time to begin the drive, day after tomorrow," J.L. said to his family that evening.

The little family was gathered at the kitchen table for supper. The evening sun spilled through the west windows lighting up areas here and there in the small house. The sun also shown directly on Maddie and J.L. thought she looked a bit like a red haired angel, if there was such a thing.

But that moment was gone when Maddie got up and closed enough of the curtain so that she wasn't being blinded. J.L. knew he would always remember the moment.

"I hate to keep the sun out but I couldn't tell if I was about to eat carrots or chicken," she said returning to the table but not before patting Jacob on the head, who seemed to have a frown growing on his face.

"John, I know you are worried about leaving us for a time, but we will be alright," she gave Jacob a reassuring smile.

"I don't want you to go," Jacob blurted out, maybe even trying to stifle a sob and a tear.

"Son, Jeffers is locked up tight. He is not going anywhere and the other two men are gone. And I wouldn't be surprised if the marshal doesn't come out and check on you. Plus the deputies, ole Swen will be by, everything will be fine."

"Pa, how long will you be gone?" The frown was still on Jacob's face.

"I expect two weeks but plan for three; we have a ways to go."

"I wish I was old enough to go with you," Jacob pined.

"You will be before you know it, and I promise, if I'm still drivin' cattle you will come with me. Soon as I'm back though we'll go to town and I'll buy us one of those new style fishing rods and reel."

"Really, Pa!" Jacob now could hardly contain his excitement; he had been eyeing the wondrous device for months in the general store window.

"And something for your mom too. I will make a good bit of money for this drive and with what Swen has been doing for me we should be in good shape for summer," J.L. said with a hopeful lift to his voice, hoping Jacob would catch on to the excitement.

"I don't care so much about something store bought, John, but the Radcliffs, up by the old fort, have a nice mare that would help us build up our herd," answered Maddie.

"Maddie, nothing would make me happier than to see you sitting smartly atop that mare. I have seen that horse and she's a beau." Then J.L. added with a smile, "Why it would be beauty on top of beauty."

Maddie smiled and said "thank-you" at this but turned back to her dinner trying to hide a blush she hadn't expected that was brightening her face.

"Pa," Jacob started, changing the subject, "you said that the preacher on Sunday was the man who saved your life, is that right?"

"Yes, son it is, but it wasn't just the man, it was his dog too. Do you remember seeing that big black dog behind the church?"

"Yeah, he was a giant!"

"I have had a little bit of memory coming back and I can remember lying out there, in a stream, half drowned and too weak to keep my head out of water," J.L. said, recounting some of the story. "It was then I felt this mouth on my shirt collar and myself being pulled out of the water. I thought I was a goner thinking maybe a bear or cougar had found me. But he wasn't growling, just pulling me out. I don't remember much after that until I was at Mrs. Valdez. I just remember glimpses of a tall man dressed in black helping me."

"I heard that the dog's name is Goliath. Isn't that a name of that giant in the Bible, Momma?" Jacob asked, peering at his mother.

"Yes, do you remember the story?" Maddie asked encouragingly.

"Yeah some fella, a boy like me, I think, kilt that Goliath fella dead with a sling shot."

"That is right! After supper why don't we look at the story together before bed and we'll learn the whole story," Maddie suggested.

Everybody helped get things cleaned up. J.L. brought in some more wood and stoked up the fire to warm up the front room and eventually the rest of the house. Maddie surprised her men with some fine snicker doodles and warm milk. They gathered together and J.L. took the old Bible down determined to read the story, but then, a little embarrassed to not know where it was in the book.

"Towards the middle, John, Samuel, the first book, I think, about chapter sixteen or seventeen," Maddie helped in a quiet voice. J.L. marveled at her knowledge of the Good Book and today it encouraged him to get to know it a little better.

J.L.'s big rough fingers pawed at the gilt edged Bible that had come from Maddie's side of the family. He tried to be careful, found the section and began to read the story of the shepherd boy, David, who would become king and the giant Philistine known as Goliath. He had heard the story before and remembered it from his childhood but tonight he read it as if it was new to him.

He read of the brashness and boldness of this giant. He read of the fear of the Hebrew people and the indecision of the king as to what to do about such a formidable foe.

He read of the little red haired shepherd boy and the confidence he had to go into battle against the brute with only five stones and a sling. He thought to himself that if David lived today that he could probably hit a squirrel at a hundred paces with his eyes closed.

He marveled too, at the humble nature of the boy who was so brave. To hear his words got him to thinking about the God this boy served and the trust he had in Him.

He continued to read, ***"'And David said to Saul, "Let no man's heart fail because of him; thy servant will go and fight with this Philistine."'"*** This was a boy, maybe not even in his teen years, J.L. marveled.

He was truly moved by David's declaration to Goliath, whose shadow alone would have swallowed David, he thought. ***"Thou comest***

to me with a sword, and a spear and with a shield; but I come to thee in the name of the Lord of hosts, the God of the armies of Israel whom thou hast defied."

After J.L. was done reading the story, Maddie asked both of them, "What did you think of that story?"

"I would have liked to have been King David; he must have been very brave," Jacob said, seeming to be deep in thought.

"Honey, he was brave, but he was brave because he knew that God was with him. Maybe you can remember that when you go out in the dark to the barn or maybe find yourself lost when you are out exploring up in the hills or when you think you see a bear. God goes before you, behind you, above you and beside you," Maddie said, trying not to preach but to reassure.

Jacob thought about that for a minute and so did J.L. They both smiled, looking like father and son. But then Maddie could see another question cross Jacob's mind.

"Hey mom, why did David have 5 stones if he knew it would only take one to do in that Goliath?" Jacob asked, obviously taking in the whole story.

J.L. hadn't thought about it, but now mentioned, he wondered that himself.

"If I remember correctly, and I think I remember the parson mentioning it one Sunday, it was because Goliath had four other brothers so he came prepared," Maddie stated, a grin playing across her face.

Both Jacob and J.L. found that funny, especially the way that Maddie said it and they had a good laugh.

"John, what did you think?" she asked.

"I thought about how big this little boy's belief or faith must have been and then I remembered a verse or at least a part of it, something like, 'if God is for us who could be against us.' Is that right, Maddie?"

"Exactly, from Romans, it means to me that there is no problem too big for us if God is on our side," Maddie answered.

J.L. knew he needed to dwell on that. He had been used to doing things on his own. He was big and strong and yet at times helpless and weak. He thought to himself, 'I guess we all have Goliath sized problems, but God is bigger and that is what David knew and maybe it's time for me to know that too.'

"David must have been a great person and he became King, right, momma? He must have been perfect," Jacob wondered aloud.

"Honey, he was a great king but he was a human being who made some bad mistakes too. He also was pursued for a long time by a man who hated him."

"You mean how Mr. Jeffers is after Pa?" Jacob asked, and then added, his face scrunched up, "I hate that man, he must be the devil hisself."

J.L. was stopped in his tracks by the harshness of his son's words and trying to think what he should say, but Maddie was quick.

"I want you to think about this: Mr. Jeffers was also born like the rest of us. God breathed life into his body and made him in His image. But Mr. Jeffers is the one who has made the bad choices that have got him where he is. Maybe we should be praying for him that he will change his ways. You read more about David and you will understand."

J.L. had gotten his thoughts, "If I hadn't been such a pig-headed fool and been doing what I was doing, maybe this would have never happened. I am the one that got into the fight with him and broke his hand to bits."

"Yeah, but those guys are the ones that almost killed you!" Jacob jumped in, in defense.

"True and they were wrong, and I guess they got their punishment for it but I can only blame myself for getting all of this started. And I am sorry about this. What it has made me understand is that we have to be a holdin' and not want to blame somebody or something else, like the liquor for me."

All thought about it for a minute, the fire lit the walls of the log cabin and danced shadows here and there. The crackling of it along with some fresh hatched crickets out side sang a little song together in the quiet of the night. Maddie reached over and gave both her men hugs.

"Time for bed, scout, tomorrow I will share more with you about David," she said to Jacob.

The family gathered together in the little lean-to section that had been added on that was Jacob's bedroom. Jacob prayed for blessings for those he knew, he even included Clint Jeffers, who was miles away thinking thoughts far from the story of David and Goliath. Jacob thanked the Lord too, for the circuit rider and his big black dog. Then they all recited the Lord's Prayer.

Chapter Twelve

His Presence

"Thou wilt show me the path of life, in thy presence is fullness of joy;
At thy right hand there are pleasures forever more."
Psalm 16:11

J.L. had much to do on the next day to get ready for the drive and to take care of things around home. Maddie and he spent time sowing grass seed in the fresh tilled ground. He made sure there was plenty of firewood ready; even though the days were warming there was still need for wood for cooking. There were animals to attend to, some fences to repair, clearing of irrigation channels down near the creek and Maddie wanted a bigger garden this year so there was a new area to plow.

Both of them spent the day together, working on all that needed to be done. Finally J.L. concentrated on all the supplies he would need for the weeks that he would be gone. He would pack carefully so that he could carry it all on Gus' back until he could shift some of it to the chuck wagon.

At the time for school to end for the day, he and Maddie took the buckboard to town to pick up Jacob and then stopped at a couple of stores to get the other supplies that would be needed at home and for him. It was a simple but busy day. Just the regular things of life but he and Maddie were content as could be, under the blue sky, to be doing this with each other.

Night fell and dinner was most welcome by them all. Jacob seemed to be gaining more of an appetite all the time while also outgrowing every piece of clothing he had.

"Pretty soon you'll be eating me out of house and home, just like you father does. No wonder every year I plan for a bigger garden," said Maddie, teasing her son.

"Too bad, mom, you can't grow penny candy, sarsaparilla and ice cream in that garden. I would be out helping you all the time," Jacob said back.

"And don't forget the licorice," J.L. added, which was his favorite. Around the dinner table was a pleasant time to top off a good and productive day.

* * *

The next morning as they gathered for breakfast, the mood was a little more somber. Jeffers, and the events that took place with him, were on everybody's mind, even though no one said anything. For J.L. it had been a night of nightmares and the war fresh on him again. Maddie had tried to comfort him during the night but sleep escaped them many hours before dawn. Maddie, however, at breakfast, took the opportunity to pray for the family over the next few weeks.

"Dear Lord, we thank Thee for thy great mercy and providence to us. Thou has kept us safe and watched over us. Thou have provided for us in thy bountiful spring, and Lord we thank Thee for that. We also bring before you Mr. Jeffers and we pray for his soul that he might see fit to seek You. But we also pray for safety for us from him if he should still seek to harm us. I pray, Lord that you watch over us as we will be separated for many days and by many miles," said Maddie quietly, head bowed.

She continued on and placed her hand on her husband's. "I thank Thee Lord for my husband's commitment to seek you. I thank Thee, Lord, for your promises to keep temptation from us. May you do so with John. I ask, Lord, for rest and safety for him out on the trail. And for us at home, Lord, help us with school work, chores and all we have to do. I thank Thee, Lord, for loving us so that we can call on you in this way. It is in Thy name that I pray for all these things. Amen."

As they ate breakfast, J.L. and Jacob talked about the trail ride and what it would entail and where it would go. J.L. reminded Jacob of the things that needed to be done. And Jacob reminded his dad that he was growing up and knew what to do.

"I know son, you have done well. I am just fussin' and being your pa," said J.L. with his big arm draped around the boy's shoulders.

Maddie had been quiet after the prayer and just seemed to pick at her breakfast and chewed on what she did eat for a long time.

"Maddie, is everything alright? You've been real quiet," J.L. asked realizing that her normal upbeat tone was now subdued.

"Yeah, it was like you were chewing your cud, Mom," Jacob said, starting to laugh.

"Actually, young man, I was ruminating or chewing some thoughts over," she said, looking up at her family. "Do you remember the story of Shadrack, Meshach and Abednego and the fiery furnace in the book of Daniel?" she asked.

"Oh yeah, those three fellas who wouldn't obey the evil king, uh, I don't think I remember his name, it's about a mile long. But anyway he threatens to throw them in a furnace so hot that even if you was a standing close to it the heat would kill you," Jacob answered back, proud that he remembered so much.

"The king, whose name was Nebuchadnezzar, did throw the three of them in the furnace," said Maddie.

"Yeah, and they didn't burn, not a bit, did they?" said Jacob, remembering more of the story from the book of Daniel.

"No, God saved them and everybody could look in the furnace and see the Lord with them."

"Yeah that's a great story but why were you thinking of that? Is it because the Lord is helping us through this fiery furnace with Mr. Jeffers hot to do bad to Pa?" Jacob considered.

"Yes, I guess so. Also I was thinking about something they said before they were thrown into the furnace. It was something like, ***"If it be so, our God who we serve is able to deliver us from the burning fiery furnace, and he will deliver us out of thine hand, O king. But if not, be it known unto thee, O king, that we will not serve thy gods, or worship the golden image which thou hast set up."*** They were prepared to die and still serve God no matter what happened."

"But what if God didn't save them, what good would that be?" Jacob asked.

"Oh God would have saved them, just not their bodies," Maddie answered.

"You mean their souls?" Jacob asked.

"Yes, these young men, boys really, not much older than you, knew that even if they died they would still be saved. Even though their bodies may burn, their souls, the true part of them, would go to be in heaven with God," Maddie was intent on helping her son to understand.

"So they didn't have to be scared!" Jacob exclaimed.

"No and neither do we. We may die and we will die someday, and I hope it is a long time from now, but we just don't know that. We do know this, that even if we die we will still live," Maddie said, finishing her thought and hoping that hit home with both Jacob and J.L.

"Well, I don't want to die either, but I ain't 'fraid of that ole Clint Jeffers anymore. He is the one who needs to be afraid," said Jacob, puffing out his chest.

J.L. had listened to all of this will little to say, he just wanted to take it all in. He was grateful to Maddie for being able to put the Bible on this and help Jacob, and he had to admit, for himself too. He was not afraid of Jeffers so much but he was fearful for his family. He finally added, "The Lord will look after us, won't he, Maddie? He has surely looked out for us up to now."

Suddenly everybody became aware of the time. J.L. hurried Jacob along because he was going to ride his own horse into town with J.L. J.L. did find time to give Maddie a big kiss and a hug which Jacob thought would go on forever. He did smile to himself, glad to see this happen.

"You be careful John, I mean it," Maddie hollered after them, then adding, "After all you belong to me, I am not done with you yet!"

J.L. and Jacob laughed, waved their hats at her and rode off following the morning sun.

In The Dalles at the school, J.L. gave Jacob a big hug and a few more instructions about being the man of the house and minding his manners and his own business. Jacob was quiet and J.L. wondered if maybe he had laid it on too much to the boy about his responsibilities.

"Is everything alright, Son?" he asked.

Jacob gave his dad another hug, quietly saying, "I love you Pop. I am glad you are back. I will be praying for you," Jacob said quietly, staring intently into his father's eyes. And with that he was gone, out of the big man's arms and running to meet his friends.

J.L. headed Gus up and away from The Dalles to the top of the bluffs towards the Flying High ranch. The sun was warm and seemed to shout spring. The wind at this moment was still, always a rarity in the gorge country.

As Gus climbed the hills that took them to the top, J.L. enjoyed the warm sun on his back and took time to thank the Lord for all that been given back to him. For the first time in a long time he was excited about life. Yes, he would miss his family and pine for them every night, however he was excited about the drive to Mitchell and the opportunity to see new country. He marveled at the Oregon country and did not think there could be a more spectacular place on the face of God's green earth.

He would be happy to be back with his co-workers from the ranch and resolute to show them and the boss that he was a changed man. He was willing to put up with whatever guff he might have to endure for becoming 'henpecked'. He was pleased to make some money to help his family do all the things that they had been talking about. All the work that went with it was actually pleasant to consider. It was as if through all of these projects the family would be building into their lives as well as their place along the banks of the Chenoweth Creek.

Upon arriving at the top of the gorge, J.L. stopped to give Gus a breather. The horse had worked up a bit of a sweat making the climb and was breathing hard. J.L. dismounted and took in the 360 degree view. He drew deep breaths of the morning air, sweet from new wildflowers and grasses pushing through the soil. A breeze wafted the aroma of the morning to him. Different from down below, the view here, revealed much of the great expanse of dense forests and white capped mountains to the west and the north. To the East the high rolling plains of the arid lands and the great sweep of the Columbia River stretched east to west.

J.L. wandered about for a few moments, kicking at rocks, watching for arrowheads and interesting stones. He knew little about all the flowers that were popping up everywhere. Maddie could tell him the names of most of them he figured. He enjoyed their beauty anyway. In some way, here, God seemed closer. Not so much that maybe he was a tad closer to the heavens but in the stillness and the freshness of the day. It was in the sounds of the birds, ravens and hawks singing in the bright day. God seemed to be in the aroma and brightness of it all. This moment was like a gift from God and if J.L. could have found a way to have embraced it, he would have. He felt happy, more than that, a sense of peace, contentment and joy that had visited him since he decided to make a new way.

On any other day he would have tarried longer but the ranch was still some miles away and there was much to be done. Soon he was back on Gus and heading off at a good clip. The same sense of joy and peace did not stay there on the edge of the gorge, it came with him.

* * *

When J.L. rode in, the ranch was a hub of activity as cowboys and cow dogs were busy cutting out complaining cows into the herd of one hundred that was going to Mitchell. J.L. directed Gus into the action helping to keep those cattle that would wander off or needed to be coaxed into the pen. Soon one hundred head were confined in one place and the others set scooting out into the range to feed on the sweet grasses that beckoned.

"Hey, boys, looks like I got here in the nick of time, you would have never got those cows together if I hadn't come along," J.L. kidded.

The ranch hands greeted him like a long lost soul but then decided on some general ribbing at his expense of him being allowed to untie the apron strings for such a trip.

Noah High had stepped out of his home and proceeded to the circle of cowboys greeting J.L. He waved a big hand at him and hollering "Howdy."

"Morning boss," said J.L. extending his hand down to shake Jonah's. "Thanks much for letting me tag along on this drive."

"You are welcome, J.L., you were the one that got this arranged. And may I say for someone who was lying at death's door a month ago you sure look like a man reborn. Are you feeling fit?" asked Noah, with real concern in his voice and taking time to spend a minute talking with J.L.

"Yes, Sir, never better. Never better in many ways. I feel like I have a new lease on life or uh, maybe a new life altogether."

"We're glad to see it. How is Maddie, pretty and ornery as ever?" Noah said with a smile.

"Yes Sir," J.L. smiled too, thinking about her last words to him.

"And that boy?" Noah continued.

"Growing like a weed, Sir," J.L. said with a smile playing on his face.

"We all had heard about that trouble with Clint Jeffers and your family," Noah said with a furrow appearing on his brow.

"We're fine sir, really and thanks for asking," J.L. reassured and feeling somewhat embarrassed. He also felt a deep sense, as if the Spirit was talking with him, 'My Son, this is what forgiveness is about. This is how I forgive you.' In the moment that J.L. had to think about it, it was like Noah didn't even remember the incident that got him fired. Was God that same way? Did He actually forget about his many sins when forgiveness was sought? He would need to mull it over more.

* * *

By noon the drive was ready to pull out, chuck wagon loaded and waiting. Old Cookie was ready to head out and complaining to all that the day was "a wasting." The noon meal was to be had first before setting out with the realization that this would be the last great meal available for some weeks to come. Everyone preparing to go on the drive ate as if it was the last meal ever.

With about five hours of daylight left the crew of six knew they wouldn't get far but the route would be to the Southeast heading towards Fifteen Mile Creek. Maybe with some luck, they might arrive there so the livestock could drink and pasture around the area for the night.

J.L. enjoyed being in the saddle again and the process of moving the cattle across the great open plain. From where he was he could drink in views of the great Northwest. He loved the sounds of the cattle and the cowboys, ponies and the chuck wagon as this noisy train of animal and humanity moved slowly along.

Out in the open space where trees were sparse, J.L. could pick out herds of deer, antelope and, now and then, a curious coyote watching but keeping his distance. There were no other people to be noticed after the first few miles of the drive.

The sun was warm on his back, almost too warm, in that clear, bright afternoon. J.L. could feel the sweat begin in the middle of his back and he wished to remove his coat but the drive would not allow him the moment to do so. Now and then a breeze would waft over him, cooling him a bit.

In this spring day, little dust was to be a bother as the barren land was now filled with green grasses, shrubs and wild flowers bursting and blooming. He didn't know how to explain it but every time the cool breeze would drift over him he would think about this God he was seeking to fill is life. He had heard much about the Holy Spirit in recent days, although he didn't quite understand the idea of God in this way but as the breeze tickled and cooled him he saw it as a relief from the heat of the day. In a similar way he thought about God. There to cool a heated brow in the heat of it and there yet as a force to chase off the frigid temperatures of the high desert night. It was surely a comfort and perhaps this was this God who was the Holy Spirit, a comforter not just in times of trouble but at all times.

The sun was now sinking low and the cowboys were watching the horizon in front of them hoping to spot Fifteen Mile Creek. Shadows were drawing longer and the warmth of the day was beginning to dissipate. No more than a quarter of a mile away, though, they could make out a line of brush and trees that signaled water and the creek they had hoped to reach. The creek wasn't much, just a ditch in the desert land where the runoff ran. Come summer you would be hard pressed to find but a trickle. Today the waters danced and gurgled as the creek serpentined across the gullied desert.

The cattle smelled the water and picked up their pace to get to it and the green grasses that surrounded its banks. Cowboy and horse took their turns at the fresh water, upstream from the herd. Soon Cookie was clanging pots and pans, getting the evening meal together. Firewood was gathered, which wasn't much but limbs and branches that had come down from the bushes and sparse trees that lined the little creek banks. J.L. did notice, as he helped find firewood, that all along the bank of the creek, wildflowers were in abundance and absolutely shimmering in the setting sun. Everytime he saw one he thought of Maddie and wished he could pick some for her.

The crew settled in for the evening, watch for the night was established and the fire was built up to warm the quickly cooling air. Out on this high plain the heat of the day was now a memory along with the blue of the day and the panorama of mountains and plains. The crew knew they would probably wake to some frost so preparations for a warm sleep were made.

Now the sky was filled with stars and so many and so bright against the moonless sky. Cowboys smoked and joked around the fire. To J.L. it was the same old stories he had heard time and time again and he would have normally been quick to add his own accounts. While he enjoyed being with his old comrades there was a larger presence that loomed in the night that kept his attention.

God seemed to be watching over everything and everywhere. The stars took on a new significance for J.L. as he pondered a Creator who threw out the starry host above him like one who would cast out a shovel full of bright sand on dark earth. Somewhere in the night the distant sound of a hoot owl called, somehow lonely. That sound accompanied the voice of the cowboy on watch as he sang low and soft to the cattle, keeping them calm in the pitch dark of the night.

J.L. continued to ponder about this God of the day and of the night. He had remembered hearing of the One who slept not and never slumbered. He thought in the same way as he and his brothers of the saddle would take turns to watch over the herd at night that God must do the same. 'God on the night shift,' he thought and the idea comforted him.

During those months of separation from Maddie and Jacob, J.L. worried the most about the night and how they would be doing against it. He would feel the guilt of his wayward life at night and think that he was not there to protect them. In that moment he could have felt the same and it was not that he wasn't concerned. He knew that Maddie could be a powerful force that was not to be underestimated but he was the man of the house and it was his job to protect. Tonight, though, J.L. recognized and had confidence that in someway, beyond his understanding, that God too worked the night shift on his family's behalf.

As the fire began to settle down into red hot coals the voices of the crew fell away to the sounds of sleep. J.L. peered at the night sky, tucked deep into his bedroll. Did God somehow live above what he saw or invisibly in the midst of the sky, he did not know. None the less, J.L. thought and felt, God's presence was everywhere to be felt that night and he realized in himself that he needed to know it the most. And in that cold night, cold points of light against the black outlines of the mountains and hills, J.L. slept content and assured.

Chapter Thirteen

The Good Shepherd

"Blessed is the man that walketh not in the counsel of the ungodly
Nor standeth in the way of sinners, nor sitteth in the seat of the scornful.
But his delight is in the law of the Lord and in his law doth he meditate day and night."
Psalm 1:1

On that same night, back in The Dalles, things were not so calm and quiet. For some reason, Deputy Caleb wondered, something had gotten into Hollerin' Howard and it wasn't even Saturday night. Howard was one of the local town drunks who managed to eke out a living with day jobs or what he could swipe in the cloak of night. With a few coins in his pocket Hollerin' Howard would wheedle out as many shots of cheap whiskey as he could. Then he would start making noise at the top of his lungs. It might be a crude limerick, off color songs and stories, hootin' and hollerin' with the idea of trying to be as disruptive as his whiskey slogged brain could contrive.

There were solitary quiet drunks who preferred to be alone and then there were the noisy boisterous ones with Howard being the loudest and the worst of all. And if he could cause some trouble, trip someone, send and insult or whatever, then it just got him going even more. Fortunately his money and the patience of others would run out quickly and he would be put into his place or perhaps the nearest horse trough for a little cooling off.

He was never dangerous and didn't seem to own a gun. During the daytime, after the hangover wore off, he was polite and hard working for whoever would give him some day work to provide for his meager subsistence. That would usually be followed by a lecture from the current employer about the need to change his ways.

Tonight, however, was different and potentially more dangerous. Howard was in the middle of Main Street with a mostly empty bottle of a brand of whiskey he would normally never be able to afford and a six shooter, with three rounds still in it. Three spent shells lay on the ground close to him and the air around him stank of freshly shot gunpowder.

One slug had shattered the front window of the mercantile store. The second had penetrated a bucket of beer being carried by a young man making a delivery. He was now shouting at Howard about how he was going to give him a beating to remember. The last slug, however, was dangerously lodged in the rump of a nearby horse that was now baying in pain and jumping around trying to dislodge the hot hornet that was in his backside and giving him such grief.

The three other horses tied to the same rail were now also panicking and being kicked by the wounded horse. The owners of the horses, local cowboys, tumbled out of a cafe and were trying to get their horses settled down. The evening was turning into a caterwaul of chaos.

Meanwhile Howard was screaming at the top of his lungs about shooting the next so and so that tried to get close to him. Everybody that knew Howard was amazed at how such a small quiet man during the day could become so loud when on the buzz.

Deputy Caleb had his hands full on what normally would have been a quiet weeknight. He would have spent most of the time in the office and jail attending to the few prisoners that were being held and making an hourly round through town. He was the only deputy on duty. Now he was making his way down to where Howard was causing all the commotion.

What was also strange about that night was Clint Jeffers actions. A curious prisoner would have been trying to get a sideways glance through the barred window that faced on a corner of a cross street, to see what was going on with Howard. Instead Jeffers was taking the thin mattresses from the bunk bed in his cell, crawling under the bed and packing the mattresses around him tightly.

"Now, Howard!" the deputy shouted, trying to shout louder than Howard, "You put that pistol down before some one gets hurt, namely you!"

Howard didn't seem to hear the deputy, he had launched into an off color limerick of which he seemed to know a million. At the same time his gun hand was waving wildly around, and he jerked off another shot, which went off above him and into a second story window of a nearby boarding house.

"Hey!" some one yelled from the broken window, "Watch yourself, or I will stop you dead in your tracks!" The man behind the voice had no intention however of showing himself as a target.

Caleb did not want to shoot ole Howard and he now guessed there were two bullets left in the pistol that he brandished, but a life could be lost tonight. There weren't many people on the street and those that were there were down on the ground or trying to hide behind anything available. Caleb had not ventured into the street but stayed in the shadows of the eave of the building on the boardwalk.

"Howard!" he tried again, "You put that pistol down or, so help me God, I will have to shoot you. Do it now before anything else gets shot up! Howard put the gun down! Drop it now! Howard do you hear me!"

"Deputy, I can't see you, but I recognize your voice. You are a fine gent, but I've got a song to sing to you." With that Howard starting singing an unrecognizable tune and began to do a little jig. He then put the whiskey bottle to his lips, still trying to dance his jig, liquid spilling out, slung it back and finished what was left.

"Whooee! Now that is whiskey! Tell you what there Deputy Caleb, I will make a trade with you, this here six shooter for another bottle of this fine sippin' whiskey," Howard shouted. And with that he hurled the empty bottle underhanded high into the air. The hand that held the pistol went up too with a try at shooting the soaring bottle.

KABOOM!! The sound filled the night air. A sound much louder than the six shooter that drunken Howard fired at the flying bottle. No, this sounded more like heavy artillery. What made up the explosion was dynamite and not Howard's pistol. The sound and the debris to follow came from the direction of the jail and reverberated in the streets and alleys of The Dalles. Dust, rock and debris fell everywhere. Everyone hit the ground including Caleb. The horses already agitated by Howard's gunfire, shrieked and jumped, some getting loose from the rails and running off down the streets.

Fortunately in that moment a man near Howard had the presence of mind to dive on him and with a heavy fist put the little man out for the night.

Caleb, who was closer to the explosion, struggled to his feet. His ears rang something terrible and he couldn't quite get his bearings. He staggered like a drunken man himself towards the alley in the direction of the explosion to investigate. Now with pistol drawn and cocked, Caleb, staying low and still struggling to keep his balance, entered into the alley. Dust was everywhere but he thought he could make out a shadow or two. However before he could even say a word or act, suddenly a frightened horse with a rider holding tight to reigns and mane tore in front of him. Caleb tried to jump back out of the way and nearly made it but a heavy boot from the rider landed squarely in his chest, smashing him to the ground and leaving him breathless. Caleb could just make out enough of the silhouette of the rider in the dust to believe it was none other than Clint Jeffers making his escape.

* * *

Will, one of the hands on the drive, who had been on watch since midnight, jostled J.L. at 4AM, "J.L. you're on and I am ready for a wink of sleep."

J.L. woke with a start, coming to realize that he had slept dreamless for hours. He hustled out of the bedroll. "I got it, Will, you hit the sack. Anything I should know about?"

"Nope, quiet as a graveyard out there, 'cept for an owl that helped keep me awake."

J.L. saddled up Gus who seemed to be less than excited about being awakened and pulled into duty. J.L. felt refreshed, the cold air woke him quickly. The strong coffee in the tin cup he balanced on the saddle horn helped too. He had come to believe, as he took another sip on the tin cup, that coffee you couldn't chew wasn't coffee at all.

He quietly circled the cattle, alert to strange shadows and noises that would tell of intruders, man or beast. His rifle, a 30-30, was loaded but the safety was on. Sunrise was a good hour or so away and yet to the East the sky was brightening at the very edges and the stars beginning to fade. A cold breeze danced at his nose and eyes making them water. He wrapped a bandana around his face to keep out the chill. Yet on this cold morning the warm presence of God, still on the night shift, reminded him all was well.

J.L. began to sing to the cattle but his voice, in the morning, was hoarse and scratchy and he thought an unpleasant sound to the ears of cattle. Instead he began to recite the only verses he could remember from long ago Sunday school memories.

"The Lord is my shepherd; I shall not want." He started out amazed that he remembered these old words from his childhood of long ago. A time before the war changed everything.

What was next he thought, ***"He maketh me to lie down in green pastures; he leadeth me besides the still waters."***

As J.L. circled the cattle he could hear the creek which was not silent yet not noisy but comforting in its' gentle rush upon rock and log. ***"He retoreth my soul; he leadeth me in the paths of righteousness for his name sake."*** He felt like a man restored and was amazed at how different he felt. A year ago, even less, his thoughts would have been else where and the Good Book he would not be reciting to cattle on the high plain.

Those words from the Psalm like ***"righteousness"*** and ***"name sake"*** were hard to comprehend but as best as he could think it meant for him to do right and that some how it was all about this God-man Jesus.

What was next he thought in that old twenty third Psalm. He couldn't believe that he would remember it and yet there it was, as if God had planted it in him as a seed long ago to come up in the new spring of his life.

"Yea, though I walk through the valley of the shadow of death, I will fear no evil for thou art with me; thy rod and thy staff they comfort me."

J.L. had seen death, more than plenty. The faces of lifeless comrades and American boys who had become each other's enemies still cast their blank stares at him to this day. 'What horror we do to each other' he often thought and yet his fists and his guns had shed blood and taken lives and he hated that such violence was within him. Could this be a place one could get through? Sometimes he thought the walls of violence could crash upon him and all those he knew. In his years in the West, while violence with the natives and settlers was less now, he had seen the evidence of it in burned out cabins and Indian settlements put to the fire.

Even in the streets of The Dalles and other villages he had been in, gunplay and bloodshed he had witnessed. Was there a way out? Who was this Good Shepherd with staff and rod that promised to be strong enough to lead the flock through and protect them?

He shuddered to think of the violence in life. The thought of it made him colder than any wind howling down the gorge in the dead of winter could do. But yet, the thought of one leading him with promise in his steps warmed him in a deep place that the cold could not get to.

"Thou preparest a table before me in the presence of mine enemies; thou anointest my head with oil; my cup runneth over." Something about coming to the supper of the Lord's with enemies about was hard to comprehend. Maybe the idea was that the long canyon of death had been conquered, like the accounts he had read about of Lewis and Clark traveling to the Pacific, under great hardship, yet coming out no worse for wear at the other end.

Somehow maybe this would be like the greatest of church potluck suppers under the oaks in summer that J.L. could ever imagine. Violence and discontent were all about, like howling wolves, but kept at a distance. Somehow there was a peace in the middle of it and the cups of joy and peace were filled and ran over.

"Surely goodness and mercy shall follow me all the days of my life and I will dwell in the house of the Lord forever."

This simple act of giving up his life to this shepherd had meant goodness and mercy. To be back with his family was the evidence of such a thing. Could this be the way of it for the rest of his days? J.L. questioned, it seeming too good to be true but . . . maybe . . . he didn't know. For this moment these wonderful things flowed through his thoughts like a pool of cool water on a hot Eastern Oregon day. And yes, he supposed, there was a heaven, this gathering place of saints and reformed sinners on a distant shore wider than the widest reach of the Columbia.

J.L. was shaken out of his reverie by the sounds of someone singing. The deep voice he heard was from some distance away. In the time that he had mulled over the Bible words the light of the new day had come to the sky and to the East the yellow and blue shades of sunrise had replaced the black night. From a distance he could see a dark rider, silhouetted against the horizon and because sound carries in the thin desert air he could hear the song too. It seemed to be that which he had just thought about and hand heard Maddie sing, "Shall we gather at the river."

The voice rang out loud, deep and melodic. A trained voice and at the same time it sounded familiar. J.L. wondered who in the world would be out here at this hour and singing such a song. Perhaps a lunatic or a saint he could only guess. It was then that he noticed that the rider was not alone but some large animal, looking like a bear, was walking along with him. It was then that J.L. realized that the man he owed his life to, and so much more, was about to ride into the camp.

J.L.'s first thought was, 'Thank you Lord,' because he had wanted so much to meet this man of the cloth and thank him proper.

The other hands had begun to stir as daylight began to break. On a cold morning like this it was easier and better to get up and moving rather than trying to find warmth in the bedroll. Besides that, nothing seemed to make Cookie happier than to throw a cast iron pot at a sleepy cowpoke who decided to tarry too long under the covers.

Cookie was up and starting out the morning in usual fashion, snorting and swearing, clanging and banging, as he set to get breakfast ready.

"What is that dadblamed caterwauling I hear?" he asked no one in particular.

"Cookie, watch your P's and Q's, the Reverend comes a calling," J.L. hollered back.

Soon the old preacher rode in, lit and with a big voice boomed, "Good morning brothers, this is the day the Lord has made, let us rejoice and be glad in it . . . and do you have any coffee?"

He was mostly greeted by silence and a few nods or looks of bewilderment.

J.L. had now settled down off Gus and went to meet the old parson, taking his hand in his paw and shaking it with gusto. "Good morning, Sir, it is good to see you but what are you doing out here?"

"Oh, I have been visiting with some folks named Emerson and I followed the creek down before I head south to a place called Mitchell. Where are you fellas headed with this fine head of cattle?" the parson replied.

"Well, as you might have it, we are headed the same way. We are taking this herd down to Brawdie in that same place," J.L. said and then asked, "And you sir?"

"I heard that there was some doings going on there and thought there might be fish to catch and sheep to lead to the Master, so I go to do the Lord's work."

By this time J.L. had found a tin cup for the old preacher and filled it with hot coffee. The old man cradled it in both hands and warming himself in front of the fire.

"You are up and going kinda early aren't you parson?" J.L. asked.

"It seems like the older you get the earlier you rise. Arthritis and rheumatism, I suppose, don't let you sleep. I am getting up so early these days, the way I'm going I'll start having to have breakfast the night before," the old preacher chuckled at himself for what he just said. "I wanted a good start, I have a way to go and there is a rare land down there I want to see again."

"Sir, would you like to have some breakfast with us? You are welcome to ride along with us. We may not travel as fast but we would appreciate your company," J.L. didn't know if he was truly speaking for anybody else but for him it seemed like a great opportunity.

"Let me give that some thought, I will certainly travel with you today, as long as I can help. I am not sure old preachers make good drivers but I could give it a try."

J.L. made a point of introducing each man to the pastor and Gideon Thomas made a point of shaking every hand and asking about each one briefly. Soon they all were gathered for breakfast; coffee, bacon, beans and biscuits made up the fare that morning as would be most mornings unless something could be hunted.

Everybody had started to eat, round the fire except the parson who asked, "Gentlemen, if you wouldn't mind, perhaps you could take off your hats for a minute and let me ask the blessing for what we are about to receive."

Many stopped chewing in mid-bite. All pulled off their hats and bowed their heads. Some thought what old Cookie prepared needed as extra blessing to make it a little more palatable. It was not a normal daily experience but there were none who wouldn't comply or complain aloud, even Cookie.

The pastor's big voice boomed out, "Lord we thank Thee that you're the Lord of all the hills and all the beasts upon them. We thank Thee for this glorious day and ask for your blessings upon us. May you give us many a mile today and done in safety. I ask, Lord, that you watch over us, each and every one. I thank-you for the life you have given us. Sustain us O Lord by your bounty and it is in your name, Jesus the Christ, I pray. Amen."

Everyone mumbled out an Amen and then tore into breakfast ready to fill up the belly and get on down the trail.

Quickly breakfast was done, camp broke and a long day of travel was underway. J.L. invited the parson to ride herd with him. It would be a good way to watch out for the old man and snatch some bits of conversation along the way.

Today they would drive the cattle south, skirt the village of Dufur and head on to the Tigh Valley so they could cross the Deschutes River at Sherars. There was a hope, however slim, that they actually might make the big river before dark. There was a good climb over Tigh Ridge and then the long winding slide down to the river. There would be little humanity but one would always be on the look out for natives on the hunt.

On this bright and sunny morning the hills were green with grass and wildflowers and vernal pools of water here and there for the cattle if the river could not be made by day's end. In fact, the task today would to be to keep the cattle moving. They would be happier to stop and eat at any given chance.

The old preacher was a good observer. As he rode along close to J.L. he would watch as the cowboys would continue to coax the cattle along. Often one or more would want to stray or stop at the next inviting puddle of water or green patch that looked too inviting to leave behind untouched.

J.L. had little opportunity to talk with the preacher but by noon Cookie found a place to stop for a quick dinner. They stopped no more than a few minutes to pull out biscuits and bacon or jerky for a sandwich and a small fire for coffee.

Off their horses and gathered around the wagon, J.L. asked the parson, "Have you been this way before?"

"Yes," the old man answered, adding, "I don't think there has been much of this country I haven't been through before although I am amazed at the size of this state and I often find myself in places that I didn't know existed. It is an amazing country, sometimes you have to look in all the nooks and crannies to find all that is special and unseen by most."

"And I recall you have been riding these ranges many years?" J.L. asked.

"Yes, any place that might have folks settled in I go, seeking to share the Good News to anyone who will listen."

"Will most people listen?" J.L. asked again of the old preacher.

"Well, most people are neighborly, glad to have some one to talk with and, yes, I think they listen for the most part. Something about this big country stirs one to think about the Creator who made it."

"You do this alone?" J.L. asked again, hoping that all these questions were not irritating.

"Most of the time, yes, but I don't ever feel alone."

"Do you have a wife back home and do you even have a home?" J.L. carried on, his curiosity getting the best of him he thought.

"I do, or perhaps, I should say I did. My Martha passed on some years ago. But I have sons and daughters, their spouses and children that I live with, over in Goldendale, on the Washington side. I travel some of Washington too. During the winter months, I don't nearly get out as much but I look forward to each spring when I start my circuit again.'

"I would think your family would fret about you," commented J.L.

"I suppose they have gotten used to it, it is what they have always known about me. They have been pestering me of late because they think maybe I'm getting too old for this. I think this is what keeps me going, the aches and the pains, even with the saddle sores, seem less than those winter days when you have to stay put. And why is it, son, that you seem familiar to me?" The old man asked as he looked at his companion. He had been wondering about this big man from the moment he had laid eyes on him.

"Well Sir, I was at that Sunday meeting in The Dalles a couple of weeks back."

"Were you one of the ones who came forward? I usually remember but my memory seems to be slipping some these days," the preacher asked.

"Sort of, that is I came forth and accepted the Lord in my heart but I couldn't quite get my feet to bring me up to the front of the church," J.L. said somewhat sheepishly. "You know me in another way and I am more than grateful to you and your dog," he added. "In The Dalles, some weeks back, your dog found me, nearly dead, in a creek and the life nearly beat out of me."

"That was you!" Gideon Thomas exclaimed. "I had wondered what had happened to that man. You must fill me in!" the preacher said sitting forward in great excitement.

"I will, Sir, when we have more than a moment because I owe my life to you and I suppose everything else too. I can't thank you enough for what you did and I want you to know that I am a changed man because of it."

There was no more time for conversation, Cookie was up in the wagon, and everyone else was mounted for the afternoon trip.

"J.L., are you coming along, or do you still need to chew the fat with the preacher?" the ramrod ribbed.

As was often the way of it, the day felt hot, the sun was high and the herd had crossed over the divide and was now on the sunny slide of the slope heading down to the river. The canyon that held the Deschutes could be seen to the east. Trees and shrubs ran like a line from west to the east marking where the White River would feed into the Deschutes. Along with the green of the fields came the soft dirt that quickly turned to mud when stepped on and everybody, man, horse and cow, concentrated on navigating the slippery stuff. Stepping through rivulets and such trying to stay mounted or on all fours on the way down was the challenge.

It was slow going, the horses would slide and cowboys would hang on for dear life while trying to keep a stubborn herd moving as they all made their way through Butler Canyon.

The crew began to realize that the best hope for this day was to settle in on the White River. Here, at this time of year, water and grass would be plentiful.

After some time and effort they came to the banks of the White River. The cattle wanted to stop but the cowboys pushed them farther down the canyon hoping to get close to the crossing before Shearer Falls. With about two hours of daylight left and a flat grassy area by the river they settled in to call it a day. Cows and horses drank deeply.

Cowboys were interested in removing boots and steeping legs and feet in the snow fed stream. Whoops and hollers were shouted as the men set bare feet into the frigid waters that rushed at and by them. They all stood in the river, the preacher too, drinking from cupped hands and soaking their heads. Suddenly fish, namely trout, began to leap from the water.

The air was full of new hatched nymphs and in the midst of the cowboys a feeding frenzy was taking place as fish leapt after the bugs. Everybody started hollering about the trout rising and leaping thinking this would be an excellent alternative to whatever Cookie might be planning for supper.

Red, a Texan who wore a large hat, swooped at the waters and nabbed a trout in the rising. The writhing rainbow had to be nearly a foot and a half long. With that catch, fishing in earnest began. Or attempts at it, if it could be called fishing, with hat in hand being used as the method. There wasn't a lot of catching as the waters were being stirred. J.L. tried his hand and hat at it too with no luck. He also kept his eye out for the preacher who was no where in the midst of them.

J.L. began to look down and then up the creek and then he saw the old man some fifty yards back up stream, in up to his knees and with a long willow switch in his hand. He seemed to be waving it back and forth. On the end of it was a thin line or string some ten feet long and on the end of that was one of the bugs. The old preacher would deftly cast the line back and forth landing the attached bug on the water here and there until there was a strike and a hook up and he would haul a large trout out of the water. He would take it to the bank, throw the fish in a gunny sack, find another bug on the water and start the process again. Goliath would bark once as if counting the sum of fish taken. It was not very long until it seemed that the gunny sack had a life of its own writhing with a full load of large, plump trout.

J.L. joined him by the bank of the creek, holding on to the gunny sack and snatching up a bug when the preacher needed one.

After a while, the preacher said, "How many do we have?" J.L. looked and counted twenty. "That should do for a feast tonight don't you think?" The two of them set about to cleaning fish. Cookie fired up a hot fire, coated the skins in lard and let them simmer on the coals. Nobody gathered there on the banks of that stream could ever remember when fish tasted so good.

Now the sun was down. Each man was filled and resting contentedly by the fire. The old preacher had been enjoying the company, the fish and now the warm fire. But J.L. could tell that he was itching to talk to the boys around the fire. J.L. though he would prompt him, "Sir, do you have some good words to share with us tonight?" He asked loud enough for all to hear.

"Well, yes I do, if it would be fine with all here," said the circuit rider as he sat more upright and reached for the Bible in his saddle bag.

Nobody really answered but nobody said no either, so Gideon took that as his cue to rise to his feet.

"Gentlemen, I don't know about you but it was a fine day for me. I greatly enjoyed your company today. I appreciated your patience in letting me help you drive the cattle today. I so much enjoyed being out in God's creation today too. What a wonderful day to be in the warm sunshine and the time with the catching of those trout. And Cookie you did an outstanding job of cooking them, they were like ambrosia."

The pastor continued moving to the subject of his devotion. "I have a question to ask of you. Like me you have come to know this country in all of its seasons. Today we enjoyed a fine day of sun and the sweetness of spring in the air, the green of the prairie and the bounty of the waters and all of those fat trout we plucked from it. However, you remember not so many months ago, when it was cold, windy and the snow lay all about and the best place to be was in the bunk house by the fire."

There were nods and mumbles of 'Yes.' One fellow piped in, "Sir, it was you who did most of the fish catching today so we are thankful to you for that and . . . huh . . . it makes up for the lack of your cowboy ways when it comes to them cattle."

Everyone had a laugh about that including the preacher.

"No, it is true; I would probably make a much better shepherd than a cow-poker." Again every one laughed.

"What I really enjoyed today was coming down the pass to see the rivers way down below, but did you notice that you really didn't see the rivers first but the vegetation that marked the banks of the White River?"

The cowboys nodded in affirmative.

"And also you know what this country looks like in August and September," the preacher continued.

"Yeah," piped in one, "dry as a bone, barren and brown."

"True, except at the banks of the rivers," the preacher said, taking the lead from the comment. "The trees are still healthy and green, full of leaves and life. The reason for that is they are next to the streams that give them life. I want to share with you, for just a few minutes before you nod off to sleep, and I am tired myself, just some thoughts about that.

I share a few words with you tonight from David's first great Psalm and here he states this, ***"Blessed is the man that walketh not in the counsel of the ungodly, nor standeth in the way of sinners, nor siteth in the seat of the scornful. But his delight is the law of the Lord and in his law doth he meditate day and night. And he shall be like a tree planted by the rivers of water that bringeth forth his fruit in his season; his leaf also shall not wither; and what he doeth shall prosper."*** If you would be so kind to me, I would like to talk with you about this tonight and if you will be gracious again let me come along tomorrow and then tomorrow night to share a little more."

"Sure, if you can catch us some more trout in the Deschutes tomorrow," piped in one cowboy, laughing as he said it.

"That is a fair deal, and based upon your fishing methods, I won't need your help," the preacher chided back. And again there was laughter.

"Now for a moment, give thought to this and may we ask a blessing on our time, let us pray. Oh heavenly Father your name is matchless and your creation shouts your name. We thank Thee today for your many blessings. I ask Lord that you watch over us tonight and through the morrow. Lord, may the words of my mouth be a blessing in your name to those who hear and may your word not go out void but be received tonight."

Everyone mumbled an 'Amen' and J.L. really felt greatly blessed by the day, he was so blessed to think that this man who saved his life would have some time to share with all of these men and for himself as well. He had much on his mind that he would like to talk about.

"Gentlemen, my question tonight is, what is your life about? Are you like that tree planted by the rivers and springs of God that gives you an abundant life and that leads you onto the life eternal in the great hereafter? Or do you sit in a desert of waste and want for that which does not add and nourish in the things that you do and the ways of your thoughts and meditations? Is your walk that of the ways of God or the walk of the ungodly in the saloons, gambling halls and brothels that often the wayward cowboy, money in his pocket, will inhabit?

And what does that wayward life wrought, but momentary pleasure and yet a great emptiness like the desert expanses on a hot August day? Do you stand with those who believe and proclaim the blessings and virtues of God or do you stand in the dens of inequity saying to your self, 'This is the life' but yet knowing in the deep recesses of your soul that this is but waste. And finally where do you sit? You may sit atop the horse and in the saddle, most days, but when in town do you sit in the pews of the church listening to the life giving words or at the poker table, in the saloons, contaminating our mind and body? And more importantly where do you stand and sit in your beliefs? Is it 'Eat, drink and be merry for tomorrow we may die' or do you think, when the night is lonely, when the trail is long and the night sky is lit with the glory of heaven, that perhaps there is more, much more, to this life that I lead?" As the preacher exhorted his voice rose in the quickening night, loud above the crash of water on rock.

"I will not bother you much more tonight but I would ask you to think upon this; 'God, the Father of us all, promises us a Living Water that we can partake in that will always satisfy and never leave us thirsty or wanting more. Our lives can be like the fruitful trees that line the shore of these great rivers or the scraggly brush that receives little and suffers much.' May the lord bless you tonight and I look forward to our day together on the morrow."

Everyone was quick to settle in for the night and many were soon snoring. The voice of the one on the watch rose up among the murmuring cattle as he sang softly some unrecognizable tune. J.L. thanked the parson for his words, he was ready for sleep too but sleep did not come too quick that night. He did not have watch so he was happy to tarry from sleep as he let his mind roam with his eyes upon the stars. He thought about his life thinking upon the words of the preacher from the Good Book.

Certainly he had spent much time in the barren wastelands of foolishness and sin, especially in the last few years and now he wondered why. What was it that drove him to nearly forsake his family and ranch to spend time in the bottle and the bad places he did?

'Why the fighting and the rebellion?' he wondered, what was it that went on within himself, as if a great civil war had taken place in his own spirit, soul, bone and flesh. He thought about his, Maddie and Jacob's place along the banks of the little Chenoweth and the trees and bushes that flourished there. Yet he could walk not too far away on his plot of land and be in a desert land where little would grow without water, tilling and care.

He didn't understand it all but he resolved to stay close to the River of God and to be that which flourished and no longer that which lived but died at the same time. His eye lids grew heavy and as J.L. prayed for his family, miles away, he thanked this Father in heaven who spread the earth like a flood with life and liberty from sin and woe and doubt.

Chapter Fourteen

The Crossing

Verily, verily I say to you.
He that heareth my word, and believeth on him that sent me, hath everlasting life, and shall not come into condemnation; but is passed from death unto life."
John 5:24

J.L. woke with a start, realizing, in that moment, that he had slept long and hard and had not budged an inch. It was still early and some of the men were up while some were trying to get a little more shuteye before another big day.

This would be a day of testing, to move cattle across the Deschutes, which would run hard from the snows of winter and the spring melt. J.L. looked over to where the preacher had made his bed. The spot was vacant, bedroll, big dog and man missing. Cookie began to clang pots and pans around and with that sound the few lazing men rose from the ground, not wanting to be caught by a flying piece of cast iron cookware for hesitating in the sack.

J.L. stirred the fire, threw a couple of pieces of wood on it and went to search for more along the banks of the White River. As he combed the bank picking up bits of wood, drift or broken branches, he noticed the parson near a rock close to the waters. He noticed that this man of God, who stood tall last night, was now on his knees, evidently in prayer. He wondered what this man would pray for and then remembered what he had said about himself, that he would make a better shepherd than a cowpoke. J.L. knew he prayed for his flock. He figured there must be hundreds of people stretched along the flanks and into the plains of the east side of the Cascades in Washington and Oregon.

He was sure that this old man of the cloth prayed for him and his comrades as well. He probably prayed little for himself other than strength and wisdom in how to be an instrument of God to these he would spend time with today. J.L. did not want to disturb this man in prayer so he moved silently away gathering sticks as he went.

As he bent down for another piece, the old pastor boomed out, "Good morning, J.L., this is the day the Lord has made and we will rejoice and be glad in it!"

"Good morning to you sir and yeah, we can do that but maybe for the crossing this morning. You might pray a little more, it could be difficult getting these cows across."

"And that I shall do, plus be of any help I might be. I look forward to this day," the old preacher said smiling like a kid on a great adventure.

Soon breakfast was done. The cattle and men were on their way, the chuck wagon clanking along in front of them. The wagon would be the first to make the crossing today and it would take everybody's effort to make sure it made it across safely. Then the cattle would come next. The cowboys would actually make two trips across a rocky bar and water so cold, to fall in it would not be to anyone's liking.

It took the herd until midmorning to reach Shearer's Crossing. Once there, Cookie directed the four horses and wagon into the cold waters in the shallowest and widest spot. The horses complained and balked but Cookie kept at them. Two cowboys rode on either side of the lead horses with lariats attached to the harnesses to help pull and persuade the horses along.

In summer, a man could walk across this spot and hardly get his legs wet any higher than his knees but today would be different. The other cowboys, that is all but the one who stayed with the herd, rode along side the wagon. They had lariats looped on to help hold the wagon upright against the current. Once in the frigid waters there was no stopping just pushing and hollering everyone along. It was a very noisy event.

As they approached the middle the cowboys on horseback found their boots submerged to above their pants and at the bellies of the horses. The wheels of the wagon sat half way in the water and at the middle of the river the wagon began to tip. Some of the cowboys chose to dismount, pushing at the wagon to keep it upright. The wagon righted itself moved a little further but then, on one end that had drifted down the current a bit, sank down and stuck fast.

J.L. was off his horse and on the downstream side of the wagon at the end pushing and lifting with all of his might. The pastor, not one to sit idly by, was off his horse and next to J.L. pushing with all of his might too. His strength was more than J.L. expected. For a second, off to his left he could see Goliath gliding through the water like a duck made for it. Everyone pushed and shoved, pulled and strained but it seemed like the wagon was stuck for good. But then the rocks moved in the water with the horses and men's effort and the wagon jerked its way out and moved on across the stream.

There was no time to think about personal comfort or discomfort in the cold waters at that moment. All the cowboys were back across the water now to lead the bawling heard of cattle across the water. Soon all were in the water, complaining as they went. The few calves that were included in the herd had the toughest time and lassos went out to pull them along.

One small calf was not to be caught and in the middle it lost its footing and began to drift down the river. J.L. threw another lasso, by luck, he believed or providence maybe, the lasso reached the calf, settled over his head. J.L. was off his horse in a split second and Gus knew what to do and pulled tight moving up and back on the river.

J.L. half waded and half swam to the bawling calf grabbing it by the neck he hauled it back against the flood. Once to Gus he set his feet on hard rock, lifted the calf on to the horse and then, somehow, managed to get aboard himself. Atop a straining horse he and the calf made their way across the river. The preacher came along side, riding close, doing what he could to keep calf and man in the saddle. The arduous crossing was accomplished and all, man and beast, were wet and breathless from it.

The sun was high and it was a good time to stop for the noon meal and to try to get clothes dry. Cowboys were soon down to their long handles and shirts and pants were draped across the warm rocks with the hope that they would mostly dry in an hour before they got back on the trail. The preacher had changed too; he came better prepared and, as promised, was doing his best to catch a meal out of the Deschutes.

With rod and another bug on the hook he began casting back and forth in some place along the bank where the water would eddy. Soon, almost instantly J.L. noted, the preacher had pulled in from the cold waters his first trout, fat and shiny. In short order there were more, perhaps a dozen in an hour's time. J.L. helped him clean the fish, wrapped them in burlap, soaked in the water and stored in the wagon ready for Cookie's magic touch for another fine supper.

Soon the boss got after the lazing cowboys, resting in the sun, "Clothes dry or not, we got to be moving on," he shouted.

From there they headed the cattle up Buck Hollow, across the little creek and up on to the Bake Oven Flat heading out across the barren plain to a new place of settlement called Cross Hollow (Now known as Shaniko). It would be the rest of this long day, moving until twilight, a night, and a full day before they would arrive at their destination. It was another new place that seemed to hint of another new town about to emerge in the burgeoning Oregon country.

That evening after supper and the pastor's devotional, J.L. and Gideon found some time for conversation, a little way from the rest, but still close to the fire as another high desert cold evening settled on them. J.L. had been waiting for this opportunity.

"Pastor Thomas, I can't thank you enough for saving my life and so much more," J.L. started. "How did you come across me?"

"Goliath and I had been out for an early morning outing, up to Pulpit Rock and beyond, just for some fresh air and a time in the morning with the Lord. We had followed the creek, Mill Creek I think, back on down and you know how dogs are. Goliath was snooping around and looking for a drink of water too, I suppose after the climb up into the hills."

Goliath herd his name at this and stirred from his sleep by his master but laid his gigantic head back down and was soon back to sleep.

"I think I could have died there if you or your dog hadn't found me."

"Yes, I believe you were at death's door. Obviously the Good Lord above was watching after you and had other plans for you."

"Do you think so?" J.L. asked, genuinely curious and wondering what being in the plans of God really meant for someone like himself.

"Pretty obvious, Son, you are here today. You seemed to be beaten so badly that just because Goliath found you didn't mean you were out of death's door."

"So what do you think God wanted to save me for? I have had no life that would want to get God's attention for any favor. I didn't deserve anything special because of my plight which was my own doing," J.L. tried to explain.

"I think that he wanted to give you back to your family. More importantly he knew that even though your life, at that point was without God, that it wouldn't always be. It is hard to say all that God has planned for you. My son, you are a trophy of grace bought with a price and I believe that God has something for you, perhaps beyond what you and I might even comprehend."

"My Missus' said you were like the Good Samaritan from the Bible, going way out of your way to take care of me," J.L. commented.

"Son, I did nothing that anybody else wouldn't have done. And we are our brother's keepers. Yes, I found you, or should I say, Goliath found you. I suppose you really owe your debt of gratitude to that kind Senora who looked after you so well. Be thankful to God for His mercy towards you."

"Yes Sir, He is the one I owe much to," J.L. said as a strange smile played across his face.

"It is true, but you can not pay back the cost He paid for you. Only be grateful and serve Him for the rest of your days."

"Well, I am not sure of what I can do. I seem to have more flaws than any one person can have," J.L. said, shaking himself back to a reality that he knew of his old self.

"The most important thing you can do is be a good husband and father to your family. Conduct your way the way God would have you. If you were to do nothing more than that, it would be enough. Your witness as a man of God, husband and father, will impress upon more people than you will ever realize," the old pastor encouraged.

"I will try, Sir. I am concerned that I cannot. I have a problem with the liquor although I have been dry for some days now but the temptation is strong and I don't know if I can overcome it. Maybe today, but I don't know about tomorrow," J.L. confided.

"Let me share a word with you, something to meditate upon as we call it a night. I don't know about you but I can hardly keep my eyes open. Here is what God says to us about temptation. ***"There hath no temptation taken you but such as is common to man; but God is faithful; who will not suffer you to be tempted above that ye are able; but will with the temptation also make a way to escape, that y may be able to bear it."***

"I am not sure I get that but it sounds promising," J.L. responded, scratching at his head.

"What God wants you to know is that there is no temptation under the sun that you face that we all may face. There is nothing new under the sun and, through the ages, all kinds of people have faced similar temptations. God wants you to understand that when the temptation comes to imbibe that you can call upon Him and He will find you a way to escape the temptation. You do not need to succumb to it. God is an ever present helper, in times of peril, there to see you though," the old man said, trying not to sound preachy but more as a comforter.

J.L. was very thoughtful to consider that. He was giving this God more and more thought and the sweet thought that He was a ready ally in the struggles and temptations of the old life was indeed good news. "You are right, Sir, that is something to give a lot of thought to. Somehow I feel stronger, more able because of what you've said. Not so much in me, but in this God that I am just learning to believe and trust in."

"I will pray for you tonight, J.L., that the Father above, who watches all our ways through this cold night, will increase your faith."

The next morning came with wind and snow flurries swirled about the drive. The sun would come out just long enough to begin to warm the cowboys but then the clouds would come in from the west bringing rain and snow mixed. The best they could all do was to trudge along and hope they would reach the Cross Hollow area that night. Not that there was much there, just a new place that people were beginning to call home. As the day faded they made out a few buildings that would become one of Oregon's newest towns. However, they stayed out in the fields, to the east, and made camp. There was new grass for the cattle to graze. The wind continued to blow and it was not much of a night for visiting. Everybody was hungry and after the evening meal, ready to hunker down in bedrolls and call it a night.

* * *

The next day came, and an inch of fine snow welcomed the cold cowboys who were quick to be up, around the fire, waiting on coffee. The old preacher had gone into the little village that night before and spent the night with some of the folks. He was back to the drive early, bringing hot hospitability from the community. There were hot biscuits, bacon and ham, some apples from a root cellar and even a couple of pies made from dried peaches. The cowboys ate it with gusto and were more than grateful to the old parson.

"I will come along with you gents for another day, then I will strike off on my own to visit some folks over on the John Day to the east," the preacher stated.

"It has been good to have you along. You have proved yourself to be a true cowpoke," the ramrod complimented.

J.L. had come along side the preacher to say, "I hope, somewhere along the line, we will meet again. Most of the time I am in The Dalles and the welcome mat is always out."

The weather cleared, the sun came out, spring returned and the little bit of snow fluff that lay upon the great plain was soon gone. Cattle settled in for the trip and it seemed like it would be an uneventful day, but as the drive headed down a grade, through a creek in a ravine, the back wheel of the chuck wagon hit hard, sunk in the mud and would not budge. Cowboys on horses latched on and pulled until the wagon was free but as they came out the wheel nut split in two and the wheel came off at the axle. Wheel and wagon came crashing to the ground. The jolt tossed Cookie from the wagon but he landed unhurt in a pile of sage brush.

The wagon, however, wasn't going anywhere. The boss called J.L. over to look at the situation because of his experience as a blacksmith. The hub nut was broken in pieces with no way to repair it. A search took place to see if another nut had been brought along and Cookie was chided by the ramrod for not thinking about extra parts. Cookie's response was less than amicable. None the less, the wagon would sit where it was until a new nut could be found and brought to the wagon.

There was new discussion about what to do. With some thirty miles to go, two more full days, they could head the cattle on over to Mitchell, pack up what they needed. Where they stopped now had grass and water that was plentiful. The old preacher offered a short cut to Mitchell that a couple of men could get through that would shorten the trip. Because Brawdie in Mitchell was a blacksmith a new part could be crafted without a lot of trouble.

The plan decided was that J.L. and the preacher would head for Mitchell, get the new nut and be back in a matter of a day or two. Then the drive could carry on.

There was an hour of daylight or so left so J.L. and the parson packed up and headed out, thinking they could get to the spot that would lead them through the John Day canyon that would short cut them to Mitchell. By nightfall, and J.L. having no idea where he was, the parson stopped them along the cliff edge that looked down on the John Day River, deep in the canyon below. They gingerly made their way down in the twilight, the shadows frequently obscuring the deer trail that they took. The moon was coming out, half in wane but bringing enough light to help in the last part of the descent. Along the banks they stopped, made a fire, found the grub that Cookie had packed for them and settled in for the night, the sound of the river stirring sleep like a lullaby.

Both men were tired but J.L.'s curiosity would keep him awake a little longer if the parson could answer a few questions.

"So where exactly are we?" he asked.

"We are on the John Day River just a few miles from a creek that will take us up and out of the canyon and across a place called the Painted Hills," he answered with a bit of excitement and wonder in his voice.

"Painted Hills, huh, is this a place that sounds like its name?" J.L. asked, his curiosity growing.

"Oh, yes and much more! I have only seen it once, coming from Mitchell, but it is a place beyond my words to share. You will just have to see it for yourself," the pastor reminisced.

"I have seen some pretty spectacular places in this Oregon country. What makes this special and how did you find out about it?" J.L. commented and asked.

"A fellow brother of the cloth, who has ridden this country, came across it. He was fascinated with the land the Lord created out here, always poking around all the nooks and crannies of this country he can find. He was told about it by the Cavalry out of old Fort The Dalles. A patrol party was out scouting and came across this place and some other unique places. Places that look like nothing anybody has seen before. They told my friend, Reverend Condon*, about these places and he has been exploring them for sometime."

"And these other places are they close by and similar?"

"Much of this borders around the John Day River and they are each unique to themselves."

"Is he still out prodding around these places?" J.L. asked regarding Condon.

"Yes, because of some fantastic finds he has made. I am afraid sometimes that it is making him more of a scientist that what he was called to be but that is between him and the Lord. He has found what is called fossils, or bones that are hard as rock, thousands of them, The bones are of animals that lived here long ago and based upon the sizes of the bones these must have been huge animals."

"You mean, like elk or something, that is a big animal?" asked J.L. trying to get his mind around what Gideon was saying.

*Thomas Condon was preacher and circuit rider who is accredited with the discovery of the John Day Fossil Beds

"Oh no, much larger and maybe like some of the animals you would find in Africa, like the elephant and camel."

"Elephants, Oregon had elephants?" J.L. asked incredulously.

"Could be, we don't know what this land may have looked liked after the flood of Noah but perhaps elephants, camels, rhinoceros and such roamed this land before the white man. In my travels I have come across rock carvings by the natives done long ago with pictures of incredible animals. Either it was something they imagined or something they saw and knew."

"Will we see some of this tomorrow?"

"Not so much here," the old preacher replied. "It is the hills that will catch you. It's like God himself took a big paint brush and dappled and streaked these hills with shades and hues of colors that you just wouldn't expect."

J.L. was captivated now, thinking what an incredible journey this was to become. And it would not be but for how he was pondering.

Chapter Fifteen

The Last Day

"And behold, I even I, do bring a flood of waters upon the earth,
to destroy all flesh, where is the breath of life,
from under heaven; and every thing that is in the earth shall die."
Genesis 6:17

J.L. could hardly wait until morning. In fact he slept fitfully. He watched the night sky, on and off, through the night, as the constellations rotated in the heavens. He watched for the bright and morning star that would herald a new day and was up stoking the coals into a fire, making coffee and being noisy enough to disturb the snoring parson's sleep. Goliath was undisturbed by the noise until he smelled bacon frying. That also brought the parson awake.

"Is the sun up yet or did I sleep all through the day and it is night again?" He teased at what was an obviously impatient J.L. "You are ready to get going aren't you, young man?"

"Well, it does sound like we do have a long day ahead of us, but I apologize, I just want to see these places. Who knows when I might get back through here again?"

Soon, the two men were mounted and on their way following a path up the river. Fish were jumping in the morning mist and J.L. imagined that the old preacher would have loved to stop and caught a few. But there was much to be done today with hopes of getting to Mitchell by the end of the day. Within the hour they came to a substantial stream flowing from the South into the river.

"This is where we head across and up. I have not taken this way but I have seen it from below," Gideon commented as he turned his horse's nose south.

It was a rocky creek and steep. Because of the spring weather, mud and muck were plentiful and so the ascent became much harder than was expected. Often the two men had to dismount, pulling at the reigns to give their horses help. The weight of the broken hub aboard Gus had him struggling. They, man and animal, would stop now and then to catch their breaths, reconnoiter their progress and consider what would be next. It took them hours to make the grade and they did not come out up on top until the sun was high indicating the noon hour.

Everyone, man and beast, were worn. J.L. and the parson slumped to the ground, sweat beaded on their foreheads and their hands and faces were muddy. Even Goliath was tired, great tongue lolling out as he panted. They all drank from the sparkling creek and soon found biscuits and such to make for their noon meal.

To the north and to the west J.L. could see the John Day running from the east. The great waters shined blue against the rocky tan colored canyon and then the greening high lands. To the south, J.L. could make out the hills that would be of what the old parson promised. From this distance he could already tell that a spectacular sight was in store.

He would have liked to have gotten up and got going then, but he knew how tired he felt. He could imagine how the old man must have felt. The sun was warm and what seemed like only a minute both men closed their eyes to rest and then to sleep. J.L. woke with a start, as he felt a prodding of a boot tip in his ribs.

"Are you going to sleep all day? It is high on to three o'clock," the parson said.

J.L. was on his feet, words of exasperation starting to flow from his mouth until he realized those were probably not the words the parson would want to hear. Or, for that fact, words he ever wanted to say again.

"Come on, Son, let's go, we should be rested up now!" the old preacher prompted.

The men were soon on their horses, also rested and refreshed from the water and grass that was plentiful at the little creek.

"Do you think there is any chance that we will get to Mitchell today?" J.L. asked, as they rode.

"I don't think so, we would be coming in the night and it is a dark canyon to go through. We should just mosey through here, enjoy what you are about to see, head out at first light and we should be in Mitchell before noon. Brawdie can probably get the hub taken care or replaced and you could be heading back to the cattle drive on the next day. Brawdie and some of the others may even want to come back with you, to help move the herd."

That sounded good to J.L. It would be nice to not have to ride hard the rest of the day. The horses would be still tired from the climb and so was he even though he had that long nap.

They followed the creek along for about five miles and as they proceeded J.L. noted that the scenery was changing. The area was full of vacant hills, but green this year from the plentiful snows that had melted and watered this arid land. The wild flowers were everywhere especially ones of a golden color that looked as if God had sprinkled the hills and valleys with gold dust.

As the creek valley opened up new sights began to emerge. Now in view were hills and hummocks that were not covered with soil or plant life. Rather, they were exposed as if someone had peeled off a layer of topsoil to show what was underneath. And what was underneath was stunning. Each hill looked like it had been used as a canvas by an unseen artist who used a broad stroke to dapple and streak the hills with different colors; reds, ocher, rusts, yellows, tan and beiges. They were an amazing collection of colors and not like any other landscape he had seen anywhere before.

The farther they rode into this valley, dotted with these painted hills, the more there was to see of them. Because it was spring, what little soil that was to be found in the nooks and crannies and around the bases of these painted hills, was where the wildflowers of gold grew. It was as if the heavenly artist as he completed his task, just for good measure, gilt edged it to make this handiwork shine.

Now and then the two men would stop and look. "I can't help but just gawk at this, this is incredible!" said J.L.

"Yes, it is as I remember it, but better because I came though in the heat of August and the wildflowers were long gone."

"You know, a long time ago, back in Virginia, before the war, I visited a great church, a cathedral, I guess. A place my Ma and Pa wanted to see. I can remember entering that place and wanting to be quiet and somehow just take it all in. It seemed like a hallowed place, where one would find God if he was looking. This place, under this great blue sky, seems just a hallowed. It is like we have visited God's workshop or paint room, I am not sure what you call it," J.L. tried to express in words what he saw and felt.

"Like his artist's studio," the preacher added with somber awe to his voice.

"Yeah, that's it!"

"We have been privileged today, to visit the Creator's studio. When you look at something like this it is hard to believe that God doesn't exist."

"I guess I have always thought there was one. I guess I thought He just wasn't real interested in what took place down here. War, I guess, does that to you."

"This says differently doesn't it?" The preacher encouraged

"Yessir it does," said J.L. thinking that the old man was stoking up for another sermon but it didn't come at that moment.

The two continued their journey, around some hills that were more dappled in yellows and tan. Here they got off and J.L. couldn't help but poke around. He felt the need to be careful where he walked because if he left a footprint he wondered how long that might stay. He prodded around a bit when a shale rock caught his eye. He picked it up and was astonished in what he saw.

"Well, would you look at this!" he exclaimed.

"What did you find, J.L.?" asked the preacher, coming up beside him.

"A rock . . . I guess, but there is the outline of a leaf on it, as if someone had pressed it into the mud."

"That, my son, is a fossil from a long ago plant that lived here."

"You know it looks like an oak leaf, but I don't see any of those trees around here, like we have back in The Dalles."

"I suspect this was a very different place after the flood, not so bone dry as it is now," said Gideon. He then added, "Which is probably why the great animals lived here too."

J.L. continued to prod around and found more, many more, of the leaf fossils. "And you think there might be animals bone or fossils there too?" he asked.

"Wouldn't be a bit surprised, they have found them not so far north of here."

J.L. would have liked to fill his saddle bags full of them to show off to Jacob and Maddie. But instead, thinking almost that it was like looting God's gallery, he settled for a few.

"Come on, we have a few more miles to go, I want to show you another place and perhaps that is where we can make our camp," the pastor said, mounting his horse.

They continued on, leaving the creek and up and over a hill. On the rise of that hill there was a new panorama to behold.

"Good Lord, Almighty!" exclaimed J.L. and then wondering about his words. 'Well,' he thought, 'it was the Good Lord Almighty who had made this so why not shout His name?'" From this vantage point a number of hills stood out. Again the top cover of these hills looked like it had been peeled off but the colors this time were reds, rust browns, cream and white. While it looked like splashes of paint, J.L. realized that it was different layers of fine rock laid, as if meticulously done, upon each other.

"How did such a thing happen?" he asked aloud, not really expecting an answer.

"I have some ideas about that, we'll talk about it round the fire tonight. I have thought about it for a long time. Old Thomas Condon got me thinking," Gideon mused.

They made camp, which was nothing more than a small fire. There wasn't much to burn but bits of dried shrub and some wood that looked as if it had laid there for a long time. They had a quick meal, but for J.L. it was hard to look at the food. Rather, his eyes wanted to wander back and forth, up and down over those painted hills.

The sun was beginning to set to the West and J.L. noticed that the hills seemed to take on another hue. As the sun dipped farther the hills that were still exposed to the sun seemed to light up in the intensity of their colors, the dark colors seemed deeper in color, the light colors bright in contrast. As if for the final touch on this amazing day, it was as if God took golden light and somehow managed to paint it invisibly in front of them and the reds, tans and whites and such were permeated with a golden glow.

J.L. took a last walk before nightfall, here and there among the hills, just to experience the changing colors in the cooling twilight. He did so for as long as light held out and until the last hill was plunged into the shadow of the coming night.

Gideon had stayed close to the fire but had watched the sunset show and J.L. as he moved about. "I have some fresh coffee going. It feels like it might be a cold one tonight," he commented to J.L. upon his return.

"Yeah, and there isn't much to burn, but let me go gather what I can find and I'll be back in a flash for that coffee," J.L. offered.

"I found some cookies in here that old Cookie must have packed for us," Gideon announced when J.L. returned with an armful of dry twigs and branches.

"That will hit the spot." And it did. J.L. did not remember when coffee and cookies ever tasted so good.

They sat for awhile sipping and chewing, J.L. would look at the fire, add some sticks now and then. He would also look back now and then, to see the hills, now dark against the star studded sky. There would be no moon tonight.

"So, Padre, what do you think?" J.L. ventured.

At first J.L. wasn't sure that the old man had heard him but evidently he was just thinking.

"There was a time, in my youth, when I would have told you, maybe there is no God at all, maybe things just got here by accident."

"Well, I don't think I ever believed that but I see your point. You go to places like Gettysburg and other battles between men and you wonder where God is. Why isn't He here and maybe you think, 'why would He want to be here among people of the same nation that have come to kill each other?'"

"Yes, I have encountered this many times and have debated it too. Here we have a God of love and we are made in His image, but like Cain slewing his brother Abel, we seem better doling out hate than love," the old preacher stated then going on to his next thought, "When I came to my senses, I came to believe God loved us so much that He made many ways for us to discover Him. When I came west, across the Great Plains, over the Rockies, down into the lands here in Eastern Oregon and Washington, I thought, more and more, about how incredible these places are. I could not imagine a greater beauty."

"By then I had come to believe in God, having come to terms regarding my misspent youth too. I discovered a Savior, the Lord Jesus Christ. My wife and I dedicated our lives to Him. We came to those out here native and white, who needed to know that God existed and that He loved them. No matter what riches they may find in this great land, it was still a smitten land compared with the riches of his glory and grace".

"As I set off on horse back to visit folks, who had found their patch of creation to live on, I would spend a lot of time getting to these places and then back. I have come to believe that what we look at are glorious places and also the absolute truth of the Bible."

J.L. was rapt upon what the old preacher was saying and every sentence seemed to create a question in his mind. But the preacher was on a roll and J.L. would have to wait for his questions.

Gideon continued on, "Everything we see, I believe, is the work of God's hand when He caused the flood of Noah to drown out the whole earth. The water must have been incredible. The Word says that the earth was some how broken up. I think what we see, as glorious as it is to see, the evidence, the wreckage, if you will, in that man had become so wicked that God had to destroy him save but for one family."

J.L. could hardly take in what he had heard. He knew he would need to think about it much, learn much more about the Holy Scriptures than he knew. There, however, was no doubt in his mind that the Hand of God had been on these places even though at this point he didn't understand the where's and why's of it.

"Sir, you have given me much to think about. I will probably stare at the stars for sometime tonight. I look forward to more from you tomorrow and the sunrise on this great place. And I thank you, Gideon, for all you have given thought to and have done."

The men began to turn in for the night. J.L. was in his bedroll first, lying on his back, looking at the stars. The old preacher had gotten into his bedroll too but within a few minutes got up again. J.L. assumed to answer nature's call but he noticed that the man moved to an area close by where a rubble of rocks offered a little bench in which he knelt. J.L. was very quiet to not disturb the man with even a shudder of sound.

The preacher seemed to be deep in prayer although J.L. could hear nothing nor did he think it acceptable to eavesdrop anyway. At times it seemed as if old Gideon's shoulders would shake up and down and, at times, he would raise his head and hands heavenward. Whatever the preacher was talking to God about it was obvious that it was an intense time for him. The preacher stayed there for a long time, long after J.L. could no longer keep his heavy eye lids open.

It would come to J.L. Matthews some time later after the terrible events of the next day how God must have been preparing Gideon Thomas. God was putting the final touch on the faithful preacher's life. He was preparing him for his trip home to heaven and to be in his presence, this unseen yet so visible God that he had served so faithfully.

Chapter Sixteen

The Day of Evil

"So when this corruptible shall have put on incorruption, and this mortal shall have put on immortality, then shall be brought to pass the saying that is written, 'Death is swallowed up in victory. O Death, where is thy sting? O grave, where is they victory?'"
1st Corinthians 15:54&55

(The reader may want to return to the first chapter to review the morning's events.)

J.L. rode Gus pretty hard, at a good speed but yet he was slowed down by the weight of a broken hub. At first Goliath didn't want to leave the gravesite and J.L. thought he would have to literally pick up the big dog and ride him along in the saddle. After some coaxing the dog seemed to sense that there was no reason to stay and he trotted off close on the heels of his dead master's horse.

J.L. then climbed out of the valley and dropped over the hill that led down to a larger creek, swollen with flow from spring melt off. He then followed along a carved out road that had seen traffic and then passed by a wagon heading downstream. J.L. inquired briefly if he was heading towards Mitchell.

Once in the little town, really more of a camp beginning to bust at the seams, J.L. quickly located the building that housed Brawdie's shop. Brawdie was there busy with the chores of a blacksmith and mayor, a number of people were there in the shop.

"J.L. is that you?" Brawdie exclaimed, as he looked up as J.L.'s shadow cast across the opening of the shop. "You are a little bit ahead of schedule. I didn't expect you all for a few more days."

"There has been a terrible thing that has happened!" J.L. blurted out but he was overcome by his grief and the shock of the morning and he sank into a nearby chair.

"J.L. what has happened?" asked Brawdie.

J.L. knew he needed to get his wits and worked to get his composure so that he could tell Brawdie and the others what had taken place. He quickly gave account of the events that led to the death of Gideon Thomas. Now he felt that time was of the essence. The wagon hub needed to be replaced and there was a hunt that needed to be mounted for the murderer of the preacher. Brawdie and the others in the shop were quick to be about what needed to be done.

"I can get a man on this repair right away," Brawdie jumped in, taking charge of the situation. "May even have it done by today." Then reconsidering his words, "We will have it done by today, I guarantee that!" he said slamming his fist into his other hand to make a point.

He continued, "We don't have the law here yet but we just can't sit by while this man gets away with his devilish deed," Brawdie said, exasperation in his voice. "We can get up a posse in no time, you can take us back and maybe we can get a sight of his trail and find him. J.L., are you up to taking us back there and see what we can stir up? It will mean a night out but as soon as this new hub is readied I will have Jed bring it out and we can head back to the drive at first light."

"I am ready to go now; a little water and I'll be fine," answered J.L., buoyed by Brawdie and the other men's concern.

Within minutes a small band of men were mounted and heading out. A big, round lady coming out of a makeshift cook tent handed J.L. a large roast beef sandwich and a fresh canteen of water. And with that the posse, Brawdie and J.L. were all off headed back into the Painted Hills.

However the day was late and sun was setting the when the little posse arrived at the place of the attack. There was little that could be done at that hour and while it was a brilliant sunset in that sacred place, J.L. noticed little of it. He, instead, found that little pile of rocks that had been the prayer bench of the old pastor on his last night. He didn't kneel there but stood and looked at it remembering how the old man had prayed in, what must have been a feverish manner.

He wondered if somehow old Gideon knew that the Lord was preparing him for his last hours. At this moment, though, to J.L. the Lord felt far away and even unreal.

Goliath found the spot were J.L. had buried Gideon earlier that day and lay down there for the night not to be motivated by food or the warmth of the campfire.

The group of men made camp for the night. The man who had been doing the repair for the wagon managed to get the job done in time and came riding in at twilight. J.L. was pleased with that, it meant that he could get the part back to the drive if he left at first light tomorrow.

It was a somber night. J.L. listened to the others gathered around the fire, especially when those who knew the circuit rider would talk endearingly of him. Mostly J.L. was quiet; he watched the fire, sipped at his coffee and just felt downcast in his spirit. He would have been happy to have spiked the coffee, on that night, with a large shot of whiskey.

He knew in his mind and spirit that somehow and someway he would exact revenge on one Clint Jeffers, who he had to believe was behind the attack. He had seen enough of his logger's style coat, red and black checked if only in a flash of recognition upon that high hill where the deadly shots were fired. He also knew he had a responsibility to the Flying High Ranch and the cattle drive to complete the task before them. Then there was his responsibility towards Maddie and Jacob to get home in a timely manner.

He felt such anger though. It was as if the one who saved his life, showed him the life, died because of his own personal sin. It was hard to bear, in fact it seemed impossible. J.L. felt that until Jeffers could be stopped anybody associated with him could be at risk. If a kindly and godly man could die at Jeffers evil hand simply because of mistaken identity, what more could happen, J.L. questioned in his sorrow and guilt?

He knew he needed to turn in and hope for sleep. He needed to be on the trail as soon as the new day would allow and he would have to hope that the posse would have some luck in finding Jeffers. He knew he needed to get back to Maddie and Jacob but what to do about Jeffers. J.L. slept fitfully. It seemed the war, Jeffers and all that was bad that had ever happened in his life had a hay day in his dreams when he did sleep.

He woke with a start as day began to break to the east. He was up and ready to go in a moment. The small party was also up and getting at the fire and coffee evidently ready to get busy for the day.

"J.L.," said Brawdie, "I want you to know we are going to look high and low for that scoundrel. We don't know him but we will be using all of our wiles to find this fella. He should not be hard to pick out. Pastor Thomas was loved in our town and we want justice to be served. I know you feel a responsibility but it really isn't about you and you got a responsibility to your boss. I am going to send Jeb along with you so you can get that part back at a good speed and then we will see you in a few days. Then we can go from there but we will be looking far and wide and hard on his trail. We know these parts better than he does. Maybe that will be our edge."

J.L. thanked Brawdie for his kindness and soon, along with a pack horse and Jeb, he set off back down the creek heading for the herd sequestered at least twenty miles away. The two men traveled hard pushing the horses to the brink of exhaustion with the hopes of arriving on that day. They stopped at the John Day River for no more than fifteen minutes for water and grain for the horse and a quick bite for themselves before pushing on.

As the sun began to set low, the camp came into sight and as soon as those in the camp saw J.L. they came running out as fast as they could.

"J.L., you alright? We been frettin' about you!" the ramrod shouted.

"I am alright, but it has been a sad day. Is there something wrong and where is Shorty?" J.L. said, noticing that he had not come running with the others.

"He is hurt bad, J.L., we were afraid to move him."

"What has happened?" said J.L. jumping from his horse.

"Clint Jeffers, bad hand and all, showed up in camp not too long after you left."

"What?" J.L. exclaimed.

"It was about dark, and he come a riding in, pistol drawn and shouting your name. Shorty was closest, he jumped in front of Jeffers' horse to try to stop him. Jeffers kicked

Shorty hard in the back and set him reeling then his horse trampled him good, stepped on his head hard. He started firing shots at us to keep us back, grazed Cookie in the shoulder. Said if we didn't produce you right away we would all die. But we would say nothing but that you was gone. He ranted and raved and tried to run over Shorty again but we all jumped at him to keep him away. He cursed and hollered and threatened us for a time but when he saw the broke wheel on the wagon I guess he put two and two together. I guess he figured you had gone on to get it fixed and headed off sniffing at your trail." By the time the ramrod was done with his discourse he was out of breath.

"Where is Shorty now?" J.L. asked, looking about but fearing the worst.

"We got him back in the wagon, I think he will be alright, he just needs a little time."

J.L. ran to the wagon expecting the worse and a couple of days ago, it probably would have looked worse but Shorty was awake and able to talk.

"J.L., I will be alright, I just feel a little busted up. A couple of days and I'll be back at it. You can move the cattle in the morning, Cookie and I will stay here, give me another day or two and I will be fine," the much bruised Shorty said, his voice raspy and his head bandaged.

J.L. quickly told all the details of the shooting of the circuit rider. And now, of course, there was no doubt in his mind of who it was behind this all. He sat amazed that evening, again lost in his thoughts, regrets and sadness, at how far this evil man would take his vengeance.

He felt trapped by his responsibilities wanting to do nothing more than seek out Jeffers and kill him dead like the rabid dog he had become. His loathing for Jeffers was only replaced for the loathing he had for himself for bringing this all on his head and now the innocent ones who had suffered or died because of Jeffers.

J.L.'s mind reeled, 'What would this scoundrel try next? Was he out there, not so far, in the shadows of night plotting his next move against me and anybody else that would get in his way? Was there a chance that the make-shift posse from Mitchell had caught up with him? Where could he be, what would be his next move?' And then just before another night of fitful sleep came, J.L. wondered where God was in all of this?

Chapter Seventeen

This Blessed Day

"Blessed are the pure in heart for they shall see God."
Matthew 5:8

The next day dawned bright and clear and the cowboys, less Shorty and Cookie, headed out across the range, staying high and to the west of the John Day River. They headed south and somewhat east with plans of driving the cattle into the Painted Hills area at Bridge Creek while avoiding the climb up the canyon. Midway in the day they found water for the cattle in a little gulch and after a short break they moved again. Bridge Creek would not be reached that day. Instead they would settle down for the night on a high windswept plain with little cover but enough spring grass to keep the cattle contented.

Another bright and shiny day came and the herd was able to settle in along Bridge Creek and follow it into the Painted Hills and settle for night at the southern edge of the geographic wonder.

As the cattle drive made their dusty way, J.L. pondered, as he watched the hills that day, if he would ever view these wonders as he had first seen them with the circuit rider. That day had been almost supernatural and God's presence seemed to be everywhere. Today, though, while the beauty of these Painted Hills shimmered in the sun, they seemed to be colored with death and woe.

He continued to ponder, the hills now slipping into the background of his sight and thoughts. If he were to ever lay his eyes on them again could that magic ever return? What a difference a day could make. How on one day God could feel so close and he could feel so blessed that he thought he might bust, to now feeling such woe and anger.

The crew continued to drive the cattle that day, up and out of the valley and then settled in for the night not more than a mile from Mitchell along the banks of the creek. J.L. went back to town with Jeb, who had stayed with them on the drive. They would seek Brawdie, if he had also returned, to tell him that the cattle had arrived.

Upon arriving in the makeshift town, J.L. and Jeb went directly to Brawdie' blacksmith shop, but it was closed. They then went to the tent that housed the saloon and café and there inside they found Brawdie and the others from the posse. They were all there and all looked as if they had eaten nothing but dust and mud for days. The men were devouring venison and ham as if they had never eaten before.

"J.L.," Brawdie shouted, rising from the table, "You made it! Did all go well?"

J.L. told him the story of what happened and then questioned, "What about you boys, did you get a scent, find anything?"

"I'd like to tell you we had him or had even stretched his neck but we did not and I am sorry about that. I believe we were on his trail and it was a zigzagging one but we seemed to always be hours away. He seemed to heading north, as best we could tell, but lost his scent and trail in a place west of here along a run of water we call Trout Creek."

Brawdie continued, "Who knows, that cur could be right behind the door for all we know. Why he would have gone to the north is anybody's guess. Maybe he is just hoping to stay out of harm's way. I guess even he knows that it's plumb mad folks lookin' for him."

J.L. was disturbed by this report, not so much that they had not caught him. He realized that was only a slim to none hope. To hear that Jeffers was now heading north bothered him.

"Is there a chance someone could show me that spot on that creek tomorrow?" J.L. ventured.

"Yes," Brawdie said, "one of us will ride out there with you. What are you thinking?"

"The drive is done and I need to get back to The Dalles. If he is heading north then I need to head towards home pronto. I might see if I can pick up on something."

"Well, stay the night here and we will get you taken care of and get the cattle in the morning. There is also a prayer meeting going on tonight . . ."

"No," J.L. interrupted, "I thank you but I don't feel much up to that."

Brawdie interjected, "It is more like a remembrance, I guess. Those that were close to old Gideon are having a little memorial and it would be good for you if you could come tonight and share about him and his last days."

J.L. agreed, reluctantly, yet realized it was the least he could do. Up the hill from the saloon was the site of a new building that would house the first church. It was far from done with bare rafters only. There was a small group of men, women and some children gathered together in what J.L. thought would be the sanctuary. There were candles and lanterns lit.

"J.L., this is Pastor William Scott and he and his family are heading up the building of this church."

Greetings were exchanged.

"Pastor Thomas was coming down to talk with us and dedicate this new place to God," explained the pastor. "So we are gathered tonight to pray for what the Lord has in store for us in our time of sorrow and thank him for the ministry of the circuit rider. If you could tell us what it was like being with him during his last days we would surely appreciate it."

At the same time as the pastor spoke to J.L. he seemed to be intent on staring at the coat that J.L. had on. J.L. realized why. He had forgotten about it himself. He still had on the circuit rider's black frock after his own coat had been ruined with the bullet that took Gideon's life.

He suddenly felt very uncomfortable and took the coat off. When he did, a few sheets of stationary fell from an inside pocket that he had not even realized were there. He stooped and picked up the papers.

"Uh, I guess, I should explain what happened, you are deserving of that," J.L. stammered out.

J.L. told the people gathered there how in the morning, minutes before Pastor Thomas' death, he had noticed that the old man had been shivering in the cold. He had simply tried to help out by taking off his coat and wrapping it around the shoulders of the old man. Gideon Thomas died because of mistaken identity at the hands of a very bad man seeking death for J.L.

"I can tell you that my time with him in these last few days was a sweet time for me," J.L. began, sharing with the new congregation gathered there. "I felt like I was sitting at the feet of one of the Lord's chosen my very self. This man was full of vigor and devotion and dearly loved the Lord and doing the work of God. He seemed to see God everywhere and especially in those Painted Hills back yonder."

"He helped me to understand things and see things from a different view. He had literally saved my life some weeks back. I . . . a . . . I really don't know what to say, to see his life snatched away before me . . . I am having trouble trying to talk." With that J.L. became silent.

"Folks," Pastor Scott spoke up, "we know we were all blessed to have Gideon in our midst and we know that as untimely as this all seems, we know Gideon went to the Lord the way he would have wanted to go, at the helm of the ministry he had been entrusted with. J.L., we are glad you are here too, you needn't feel bad one bit about what has happened.

Evil is everywhere. We would sure appreciate it, if you might read what is in those papers to us, if it's appropriate."

"Well, I guess I could do that. Uh, let me look," J.L. said, opening up the papers. The few sheets were written in neatly done longhand. The letter or sermon started out 'My fellow brothers and sisters in the Lord.' J.L. felt that it was all right then to share this with these folks who this must have been written for.

"It seems," J.L. started, "that this must have been written just for you. This must be the dedication and I feel honored, yet lacking, to read it to you. But this I will do."

J.L. began reading the last words of Pastor Gideon Thomas, "My fellow brothers and sisters in the Lord, we are gathered here today in the sight of the One who has ordained this house of worship to be built and to dedicate these premises to Him, our loving and good Savior, Jesus the Christ.

And like the Apostle Paul, as he saw churches spring up all around him, I give thanks to God for you, the saints gathered here in Mitchell, called to live the righteous life of the Christian before God and man.

This is a hallowed and holy day and I am of great privilege to share it with you and I thank ye for asking me to serve you in this way. It is no small feat, in human effort, to do such a task as to build a church and begin a new work. We know, as has been most evident to us, that this is the will of the Father of us all and the One who gives us the Holy Church.

What great things you will see in the years to come. This place of timber, shingle and glass that make up this building will indeed become like a lighthouse shining it's light out in this sea of sagebrush and new humanity.

We dedicate this building on this day to the Lord and may His lamp-stand burn bright and may the Holy Spirit always be the Governor and promoter of this work. In my flesh I hope to visit you many times but the truth of the matter is, our time is God's and I feel called more towards my heavenly home every new day."

As J.L. read the letter he was blessed to hear what he read but was also amazed at his own voice, deep and resonant, the more he read. He had never felt comfortable speaking aloud or in public settings, but there was something about doing this that warmed his heart in a way he could not understand or explain.

J.L. continued, "God has made a way for His beloved. He too had to leave those He loved and who had received Him. In this way He makes plans for us and I, like Paul, love to be in the work of it. Yet, I desire to be with my Creator and Savior and to see my blessed wife and loved ones again. This is a new work and I am an old one, wearing out like an old clock but ready for the new life promised."

J.L. continued to read and, in someway, even though he had never read those words before, they became his to share. The letter continued on with other endearments to the Lord and exhortations to the believers in Mitchell. What J.L. marveled was how this man, now gone to his reward, was accepting that he was in God's hands and in his hands he rested and was ready to leave for heaven in them.

It was of a help to know that while God may have never chosen to utilize Jeffers' deed yet in some way he made use of it for his greater purpose. This assurance, however in his humanness and newness to the Lord, did not quell his growing anger and sense of responsibility to stop Jeffers in his tracks before more harm was done.

At the end of his reading, all that were gathered there were caught in great emotion about what they had heard and the circumstances that brought this strange day to be. Here was a stranger in their midst, a dear loved one now lost and yet although gone, Gideon had his opportunity to share once more because of this stranger. It was bittersweet.

"J.L.," pastor Scott said, "we cannot thank you enough for telling us of Brother Thomas' time with you and sharing his letter so eloquently with us."

"Sir, and all of you gathered here," J.L. started, "maybe there could be no greater pleasure for me than this, other than to be able to hear that man's great voice again. I thank you for your kindness, and even though I know little about this church business, I wish you the best."

With that J.L. started to leave. Pastor Scott followed him out of the building. "Brother J.L.," he said, "I know this has been hard on you, but remember that God knows what needs to be done. Today, to hear you read these words to us, was no accident. I think the Lord has work and purpose for you beyond what you might imagine. Don't be surprised to find yourself someday doing a similar work, that of the circuit rider. Lord knows this country needs more like Gideon in the worst of ways."

J.L. replied back, bothered and yet intrigued by the pastor's comments. "I have family back in The Dalles that needs me and somehow this bad business with Jeffers must come to an end and soon. I appreciate your kind words and I know you will be praying for me because I can see it in you, but you are dead wrong about me ever being a circuit rider or anything as fine as God calls some to be."

Chapter Eighteen

Back Home

Jesus answered and said unto him.
"If a man love me, he will keep my words; and my Father will love him,
And will come unto him, and make our abode with him."
John 14:23

J.L. rode the mile back along the creek to where the cattle and men were gathered for the night. Goliath greeted him like he was a long lost friend and J.L. was glad to give the big dog a good petting. He then proceeded directly to find the ramrod. He was at the camp fire where the others had gathered all yawning and finishing the last of the coffee.

"J.L. you are back and you look like you got something on your mind," said the ramrod.

"I would like to leave at first light. I know it may do no good but I got to see if I can get a scent of Jeffers' trail. One of the men from Mitchell will ride out with me in the morning to where they think he headed north. I also need to know that my family is safe. Who knows what Jeffers has up his sleeve next," J.L. explained.

"You don't worry about us, but you watch your back and make good time to that family of yours. I reckon they and you will feel better, being together," the ramrod nodded in agreement.

Before first light J.L. was mounted and on his way back to Mitchell. He was consumed with his thoughts and he really didn't notice that Goliath was following right along with him. Once in town J.L. went straight to Brawdie's shop. The doors were open. Brawdie had a fire going and coffee on. Charlie, the one who was to show him out to Trout Creek, was there and ready. J.L. thanked Brawdie for his help and soon he and Charlie were on their way.

They moved at a good clip because it was near a half day's ride just to get to the creek where the tracks had been spotted. Goliath kept up as best he could with the horses although he was definitely exerting strength to do so.

"That is quite the dog you have there, J.L.," Charlie commented.

"Well, he is not my dog, but he was old Gideon's. I guess he just seems the need to be with me and I am not sure how to tell him no. Besides if it weren't for him, I know I would not be talking with you today."

By noon the two men had found the little creek that was meandering across the desert highland running north. They stopped to let the horses and Goliath drink and then took their turns to drink and top off canteens in the cold stream.

"Ain't much to show you here, J.L., we just noticed fresh shod track here but that has now been days ago. It could be somebody else too, I reckon, but I'm a guessin' not. I wish you all the luck in the world to find your prey. I hope that hombre gets his neck stretched good or put out of his misery with a slug. Be careful, he ain't worth you losing your life for," Charlie encouraged.

J.L. thanked Charlie for his kindness and said goodbye but was immediately about tracking the prints and on his way down the creek. Every now and then the tracks would be lost as evidently the rider would cross the stream to proceed up the other side when it would be easier to navigate or perhaps throw off those that might be on his tail.

As the day began to draw to a close, the tracks became indiscernible again. A herd of antelope had evidently been through after the rider and had obliterated any sign of his trail for some length. The herd had evidently stayed near the creek making their way north too.

J.L. could do nothing more that night than make camp which was nothing more than a small faire beside the creek. Gus found enough grass to eat plus a handful of oats that J.L. offered. J.L. shared his supper of jerky and biscuits with Goliath. The starlit night sky found the two, dog and man, stretched out together under the stars. Goliath was not content to lie anywhere else but besides the man with his giant head resting on J.L.'s chest. J.L. did not mind and appreciated the warmth. Sleep came to them quickly.

The next day was fruitless and without event, just man, horse and dog making their way north. By day's end they had reached the spot that the cattle drive had camped near to Cross Hollow. It was the same place that Gideon had gone to and spent the night with kindly folks who had provided a much improved breakfast for the cowboys.

J.L. wondered if he could find these folks, let them know what had happened to the preacher and ask if the likes of Jeffers had been seen. This place was another out of the way settlement sitting high on the plain. People had begun to establish farms and homes because there was water and range.

As he proceeded along north and west he spotted a large herd of sheep and a ranch. He made his way in the twilight, shouting out "Hello to the house" before he got too close. A man hauling firewood in for the night spotted J.L. from the woodshed. "Evening, what brings you to these parts and at this time of day? You don't look familiar to me."

"Matthews is my name," said J.L., extending his hand down but not yet dismounting from Gus. Goliath was not so polite and was eager to say hello. "I ride for the Flying High ranch out of The Dalles. We were through here some days back with a herd of cattle. We were traveling with a preacher name Thomas, you know of him?"

"Yep, sure do, he spent the night with us," the man answered back.

"Then you are the kind folks I was hoping to find, that provided the vittles for us."

"Yes, in part. Others helped but that was my wife, best biscuit maker around. Which I guess ain't saying much since there's not many of us around but I'll take her biscuits any day. Are you traveling back and where are your pards?"

"Sir, I have a sad story to tell you," said J.L., dismounting.

J.L. was invited into the home of Jonathon and Constance Moore and their two daughters. He thought the girls to be in the mid-teens. The young ladies and Goliath had obviously become friends before and he was now content to take up their attention.

"I hate to tell you this folks, but Gideon is dead. I suppose he has gone on to heaven." J.L. told the story and it was obvious that this family knew Gideon. The women, all three were crying softly and Mr. Moore was trying to find a way to console everybody with words that didn't seem to help much.

"I am very sorry to tell you this, but I am on the trail of the man who shot old Gideon because that bullet was meant for me. What I am wondering is if you have seen a stranger in the last couple of days that is favoring a bandaged right hand. Probably traveling alone, wearing a red and black logger's coat," J.L. asked.

At that the family came alert, now thinking about this.

"Yes, said Mrs. Moore, "that very man was through here no more than . . . when was that, yesterday. He came in to our ranch around dinner time. Helped himself to the water trough, himself and his horse, without so much as a 'how do you do' first."

One of the young ladies chirped in, "Gave me the creeps and he was dirty and I didn't like the way he looked at us."

"I was at the house," Mr. Moore added, "I am glad I was because he didn't look the type that I wanted around my girls if I had hadn't been here. He said he was hungry and we gave him some bread and mutton and we wished him well and set him on his way but we were glad to see him go."

"At first I was going to offer to look at his hand." Mrs. Moore said, "But my concern of him overtook my Christian duty and besides he had one of the biggest rifles I have ever seen."

"What kind of rifle?" J.L. asked.

"I couldn't quite tell, but it looked like a large caliber like what they used back in the days of the buffalo hunts," Mr. Moore answered.

"And are you saying that was yesterday, around the noon hour? And which way did he head off?" J.L. continued to inquire.

"He was going north, didn't say where he was heading but that was the way he went."

"Folks, you met up with none other than Clint Jeffers who took the preacher's life. I need to be pressing on. Maybe if you could spare a little grain for the horse and if you have some leftovers about for this big dog, he has been living on little the last couple of days"

The family got busy. Gus and Goliath were both fed. J.L. wasn't going to sit and visit but stayed on his feet wishing to mount up and travel through the night.

"You are more than welcome to stay with us this night," Mr. Moore offered, "but it looks like you have plans to move on shortly."

J.L. nodded in agreement and the couple knew that no amount of offered hospitality would change this stranger's mind.

While the horse and the dog finished up, the women of the house quickly wrapped biscuits and mutton in brown paper and gave it to J.L. "You need your strength, Sir, and be careful and we will be praying for," Mrs. Moore comforted.

J.L. headed across the plain in the dark, a quarter moon against a cloudless sky, helped him stay on the rough road that ran north. He knew that while he may not catch up to Jeffers today that probably tomorrow he would be home and that thought kept him awake and prodding Gus along. He also had to believe that Jeffers must be headed back to The Dalles too although, in his way of thinking, it made no sense. But then none of this made any sense.

Just before dawn, J.L. jumped with a start at a nicker that the horse made. He realized that Gus had stopped moving and that he had actually nodded off in the saddle. Goliath lay under a big juniper tree on some new grass. Near them the sound of the Deschutes River could be heard. Gus had traveled all night making good miles and now waited patiently for J.L. to waken. He lit off the tired horse, stripped off saddle and blanket and Gus headed for the stream. J.L. decided that a stretch was necessary and lay down by Goliath, covered himself with the horse blanket and fell back to sleep. He woke a couple of hours later, Goliath's head once again resting on his chest. The sun was bright, the day would be warm and there were some miles to make but J.L. would get home that night no matter what.

* * *

The day was getting long on to being done. But he had now picked up on the Chenoweth Creek high in the hills above the gorge. The sun was setting; turning the snow capped peaks, to the west and north, pink Even the Columbia, in that bright warm twilight was splashed with pink as well as the green hills, which seemed to just glow. He noticed below, coming around the Chenoweth Cliffs that his home nestled along the banks of the little creek, never looked more inviting.

Maddie was still outdoors finishing up taking the laundry down that had been hung to dry.

"Is that you, are you home?" Maddie shouted when she saw her husband riding in on the far side of twilight.

"None other," J.L. shouted back, "but I am tired and ready to be off ole Gus who likely has the same thought. We have come a far piece today."

"Did you ride in with the others?" Maddie asked, wondering about the cowboys from the Flying High ranch.

"No," said J.L. dismounting with some difficulty, stiff from the long ride. "They are not far behind me, probably another day. I have a story to tell you though. But are you both alright, has anything happened" J.L. questioned and looking around for Jacob.

"Oh, John, we have been so worried, Jeffers has escaped."

"Maddie, I am afraid I know that and he came looking for me."

"Are you alright?" Maddie said, looking her husband over, seeing if he had been hurt again. She had her hands on him and putting her arms about him while giving him a quick inspection for injuries.

"I am fine, I guess, but it is another story for Pastor Thomas."

"Pastor Thomas? You mean the circuit rider? And isn't that his dog?" Maddie asked, Goliath was drinking from the horse trough like it was the last water he would ever see.

"Yep, the very same, the old preacher who found me. We met up with him along the trail. Then we had a breakdown with the wagon and Gideon and I set out for Mitchell through a place called the Painted Hills."

J.L. was trying to capsulate the account. "It was there we met up with Jeffers, although I never laid eyes on him. But he shot Gideon dead and I have been on his trail and my way back these last few days. Has anything happened here?"

"No, no, John, we have been fine, we have kept our eye out but nothing has happened," said Maddie, then adding, "but why would Jeffers shoot the pastor?"

"I will tell you the whole story but I am glad you are all fine," said J.L., feeling a great sense of relief. It was at this moment the wear of the long ride overtook him and he was amazed at how weary he felt. He slumped down on the steps of the little house. Jacob then appeared from inside the barn, evidently attending to chickens and such.

"Pa!" he shouted, running to his father who swept him into his arms giving the boy a big bear huge with the last of his strength.

"Jacob, let your father rest a moment," said Maddie, thinking about what she could do next for weary husband.

Soon J.L. lay in the old tub in the barn, warm and soaking in soapy water. Jacob gave his dad's back a good scrubbing with the brush and made conversation about this and that and what had been happening through the eyes of a young boy. J.L. was glad to hear his son and it didn't matter so much what he was saying he was just glad to hear him.

Supper was hot and tasty and the fire in the fireplace a comfort. The fire wasn't really needed but for cooking because the weather was mild, it felt good anyway. Soon the family of three was tucked into beds. J.L. could not remember Maddie feeling more of a comfort to him, her head upon his chest. Goliath, on the other hand, seemed to be happy to adopt Jacob as his own although he wasn't very good at sharing the boys' small bed.

As J.L. drifted off he felt a sense that, somehow, all was well, at least for the moment and he could truly rest. What tomorrow might bring he would concern himself with tomorrow. He knew that very soon he would need to go over to Goldendale to visit Gideon's family and home church. Tonight, there seemed no better place to be than home. There was still the present matter of the murderous Jeffers and what to do and he would need to let the marshal know of the happening tomorrow first off.

* * *

A day and a night later, and not too many miles away, in the dead of night, after midnight, two men sat in a dark room lit only by a small fire in a huge fireplace. The only other light was a dimly lit lamp on a large mahogany desk. The room they sat in was the well appointed room of a wealthy man. The study, lined with book shelves and rich furnishings, spoke of power and fortune. The little fire danced dark shadows off these trappings of wealth and somehow made the room look and feel sinister and evil. The two men were talking quietly but not secretly, an open bottle of an expensive whiskey sat on the desk. As the men would talk, they would sip.

"Tell me again, how you missed with Matthews, this is too fantastic to believe," said the small elderly man.

"I will tell you again. I tracked Matthews to a place called the Painted Hills. I had him in my sights from the night before but I could never get off a shot. During the night this big dog seemed to have got my scent and I had to move farther up this hill from where they were camping. I woke early but they were up before I was and still at their camp."

"Why did you sleep anyway?" the small man was becoming agitated, his voice raising.

"I tried not to but I was so worn from hoofing it trying to find Matthews that I just slipped off. No matter, I woke in time to see the two mount up. It was still dark but the sun was breaking and kinda in my eyes but, I swear, I could make the two out. I knew it was Matthews by his coat so I took my shot. He wears that old coat from the war. I got him in my sights, dropped him like a deer and shot off another to keep the other fella down. I hit him and I kilt him dead, I know I did!"

"Then you tell me this you blind bat, who did you kill? Because I will tell you who you didn't kill! You didn't kill J.L. Matthews! I saw him, his wife and that brat of a boy ride into town as alive as you and me today!!" the little man was nearly shrieking.

"And who you did kill was a preacher man who was much loved in these parts and there will be hell to pay and not by me but by you if you don't do what I paid you to do!" the little man continued, voice raised and words sputtering out in ire.

Clint Jeffers muttered a spew of obscenities, tossed back the rest of the whiskey in his glass and started to rise.

"Sit down! We are not done, not by a long shot! I don't care what you do, how you do it. I don't care if you kill the whole lot of them, but I want it done and done quick! Do you hear me? I will put your miserable carcass down and leave you for the buzzards which probably won't touch you on a bet!!"

"I will get it done, I vow it on my ma's grave," Jeffers said, trying to exert his voice against the other.

"Jeffers, I doubt you had a mother. Now you will get it done and soon or you will have hell to pay and you can dance to the hangman's noose all the way to the devil's front door!"

THE END

The New Beginning

Dennis Ellingson has served as a pastor and a counselor. He is the author of "God's Healing Herbs", "God's Wild Herbs" and, along with his wife, Kit, "The Godly Grandparent". Dennis is a born and raised Oregonian who loves to explore God's creation in the Oregon land, East of the Cascades. He and Kit reside in beautiful scenic Southern Oregon.

All photographs are by Kit Ellingson, taken in and around the Columbia Gorge country and high desert lands of The Dalles, The Painted Hills National Monument and other East of the Cascades locales.

Comfort Inn

888-751-9848

Hwy-5 Galt / Lodi

99 + 277

($124 + tax) King - 1 Night

7-16

* 6000 points for free night

209-744-7800 - direct #

conf

2094 8922

6light

3Q 3W1H

CPSIA information can be obtained at www.ICGtesting.com
Printed in the USA
BVOW020202280912

301604BV00001B/2/P